COLD GROUND GINGER

Ginger Lightley Cozy Mystery Series - Book 3

ROBERT BURTON ROBINSON

COLD GROUND GINGER

Robert Burton Robinson

Copyright © 2017 Robert Burton Robinson

This book is a work of fiction. Names, characters, places, and incidents are either products of the author's imagination or used fictitiously. Any resemblance to actual events, locales, or persons, living or dead, is entirely coincidental. All rights reserved. No part of this publication can be reproduced or transmitted in any form or by any means, electronic or mechanical, without permission in writing from the author.

Copy Editing by Always Write
www.alwayswrite.us

Cover images:
http://www.istockphoto.com/vector/spooky-grave-gm156032623-22072703
https://us.fotolia.com/id/59716437

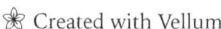 Created with Vellum

To Betty Jean Pinson
Thank you for reading to me when I was a kid,
and for teaching me how to love and laugh.
I love you, Mom.

ROBERT BURTON ROBINSON'S COMPLETE BIBLIOGRAPHY

Ginger Lightley Cozy Mystery Series
Sweet Ginger Poison
Ginger Dead House
Cold Ground Ginger

Nightmares of a Novelist (Four Short Stories)
Four Steps Under (Psychological Suspense)
Deadly Commitment (Thriller)
Dream Tunnel (Kids Sci-Fi)
Rebecca Ranghorn - Texas P.I. (Mystery)

Greg Tenorly Suspense Series
Bicycle Shop Murder
Hideaway Hospital Murders
Illusion of Luck
Fly the Rain

Visit the author's website:
RobertBurtonRobinson.com

ACKNOWLEDGEMENT

Lynda,
Thank you for your constant love and encouragement.
I love you, baby.

CHAPTER ONE

Coreyville, Texas—near Longview
Wednesday, March 23, 2016
10:55 p.m.

*G*inger Lightley's flashlight flickered as she hurried across her back yard to the cemetery gate. When she touched the cold metal latch, a chill shot up her arm. A flurry of cool wind blew up her dress and apron, and she struggled to push them back down. She wished she'd taken the time to put on her winter coat before stepping out of her warm kitchen, but there was no time to go back for it.

Susanna Clampford, a woman in her mid-sixties, like Ginger, was somewhere out there in the black night among the graves, either lost or injured. When she'd called Ginger a few minutes earlier and said she was walking to Ginger's house from Coreyville Hotel by way of the cemetery shortcut, Susanna's phone had gone dead in the middle of the conversation. Either her phone lost service at that moment, or she'd dropped it or fallen down. Ginger had called her back, but it went to voicemail.

She opened the gate and it squeaked, reminding her once again that she still hadn't oiled the hinges. Her eighty-eight-year-old neighbor, Mrs. Martin, a retired elementary school principal, had the hearing and the bark of a chihuahua, and every time she heard the metal-on-metal squeal, she would run to her kitchen window, press her face to the glass, and yelp her disapproval. At this time of night, if Ginger woke her up, the crabby old woman would probably try to call in a SWAT team.

Ginger studied Mrs. Martin's house. All of the windows were still dark. Apparently, she was a heavy sleeper. Maybe she was snoring like a freight train and couldn't hear anything else. Ginger closed the gate behind her and latched it securely to make sure the wind couldn't blow it free and hammer it against the fence like a bell clapper. No need to press her luck with Mrs. Martin.

She began walking along the familiar trail that led from her back yard to the alley behind her bakery. She used it nearly every day, except when the ground was wet and muddy, so she could stop and have a chat with Lester. It had been six years, and Ginger was now sixty-six. Lester was still sixty-two, and always would be.

She called out, "Susanna? Susanna? It's Ginger. Can you hear me?"

The only answer was a gentle breeze whistling a soft, eerie melody through the treetops.

Ginger was now beyond the glow of her porch light, and there was not even a hint of moonlight.

A cold gust of wind surprised her, throwing her off

balance, and she collided with a low tree branch.

Old Coreyville Cemetery was not being managed the way it once was, and Ginger had been complaining about the maintenance of the trees and shrubbery.

Her hair blew to one side, and she shivered as she untangled herself from the tree branch.

Her flashlight went out.

Suddenly the wind stopped. The air was dead still.

She hit the side of her flashlight with her hand, and it came back to life, but the beam was weak. The batteries were dying fast. She could see where she was about to step, but no farther.

Ginger took it slow, wanting to find Susanna as quickly as possible but knowing that she'd be no help to anyone if she tripped on a branch or some other windblown object and became immobilized. The two of them would be crying out to each other for help, with no one to answer. However, Ginger had her phone in her pocket, and unlike the flashlight, it still had plenty of power. And if her flashlight went dead before she located Susanna, she could use the flashlight app on her phone to find her way home.

This was crazy, though. Wandering around in a cold, dark cemetery with a weak flashlight and no coat? She could just take out her phone, call 9-1-1, and go back to her warm house. Let the police come out with their powerful flashlights and bullhorns and dogs. They could track her down in no time. Of course, it would probably take them at least ten minutes to arrive. Ginger could find her faster than that.

Besides, what if this was a prank? Would Susanna do that to her? Yes, she just might. Then Ginger would look like a fool for calling in the cops.

She began walking again. Her nose picked up the strong scent of Japanese honeysuckle. It was a lovely aroma, but almost too much for Ginger. Her acute sense of smell and taste had helped her create dozens of tasty cake recipes and earned her the Queen of East Texas Bakers moniker, but sometimes she wished she could turn down the sensitivity level just a bit.

She yelled, "Susanna? Susanna?"

Why wasn't she answering? If Susanna had taken a wrong turn, she might be way in the back of the cemetery. Perhaps she'd fallen and hit her head and was badly injured. What if she was dead? Nobody liked Susanna, least of all Ginger, but she'd forgiven Susanna for what she'd done—or at least she thought she had, until she began to dwell on it again. Why couldn't she just let it go once and for all?

Because Susanna was despicable.

Quit that!

What if she had to give Susanna CPR to bring her back to life? Ginger would do it, of course. Whatever it took. But they would never be friends. How could they be, as long as Susanna treated Ginger as her mortal enemy—as though it were a fight to the death between them and their two bakeries.

She shouted, "Susanna? Where are you?" Ginger heard the frustration in her own voice. It was not something she wanted Susanna to hear, sounding like she hated to be bothered by someone who might be in dire need of her help. "Susanna? Are you okay, honey? Please answer if you can."

It was the first day of Ginger's annual bake-off, a four-day event that she held in conjunction with the final week of the Coreyville Carnival. The carnival was held at the fairgrounds, located at the edge of town, just a few blocks from Ginger's bakery, Coreyville Coffee Cakes.

Ginger's bake-off was a great promotional opportunity for the participating bakeries because it attracted folks from all over the area, including Longview, Marshall, Gladewater, and Tyler. She had kicked things off with an orientation dinner that evening. For the next two days, contestants from eight area bakeries would be giving lessons and schmoozing with fans at Coreyville Hotel, and then selling their cakes and pastries from tents at the carnival. Ginger marveled at the very idea that bakers could have fans.

On Saturday, at the carnival, judges would select the three winning cakes. And the competition was brutal. Every baker lusted after the first-place trophy that Ginger had won every year.

"Susanna?"

Ginger heard something up ahead. Probably an armadillo or a raccoon. The type of critters that roamed the cemetery usually stayed clear of humans as long as they didn't feel threatened. Ginger would never forget the time she'd accidentally walked into the safe space of a nervous skunk. She thought her nose was going to explode. Couldn't smell anything but skunk for a week.

"Susanna?"

She noticed a light in the distance, and hurried toward it. "Susanna?"

The light was on the ground. Susanna had apparently fallen and dropped her flashlight.

When she got closer, though, she didn't see Susanna. There was only a flashlight, jammed into the ground at the back end. The beam was directed at Ginger's gravestone, which stood beside Lester's.

Ginger leaned over to get a closer look. She could smell the plastic of the flashlight and just a hint of something else—an unexpected scent. It was—

She froze as she saw something shocking.

The date of death had been added to her gravestone.

March 23, 2016.

"That's today," she said out loud.

She was still bent over when she heard something behind her and turned her head to look.

A woman towered over her.

Short, blond hair.

A bat in her hands—no, a shovel.

Susanna?!

She wasn't in distress at all.

She wasn't lost in the cemetery.

The whole thing was a trick, a ruse, to lure Ginger out there so she could attack her.

This was the last straw! No more valiant attempts at forgiveness.

This was war!

Before she could move, the shovel struck the side of her head.

Ginger felt the energy draining from her body.

She needed to get up.

The next blow could crack her head wide open.

But she was too weak. She was helpless, about to pass out.

Or was she already becoming brain dead?

Was Susanna about to strike her again?

Hundreds of thoughts flashed through her mind in less

than a second. So, this was how she would die? With a red-hot hatred burning in her heart? She'd always assumed that when the day came, she would go peacefully—maybe like Lester, in her sleep—or at least with a calm, loving heart. But all she wanted to do was get up, snatch the shovel out of Susanna's deceitful hands, and beat her to death with it.

What a grisly thought to die with.

She pictured Lester, who was buried just a few feet from her. They'd always talked about him taking an early retirement, buying an RV, and touring the country. Ginger had great employees, and she could have taken off for weeks at a time. But then Lester was diagnosed with lung cancer and went down much faster than the doctor had predicted. He didn't even smoke. Perhaps it had been caused by working at the chemical plant for all those years.

She and Lester never bought that RV. They never went anywhere but the doctor's office and the hospital. And finally, to the funeral home.

But recently, Ginger had been given a second chance at love. She and Elijah Bideman had been inching toward marriage. Now that dream was dying too.

Her one happy thought was that she'd soon be joining Lester, her mom and dad, and her Grandma Jessie and Grandpa Cecil. Ginger missed them all so much.

It seemed to be happening in slow motion. She fell forward until the top of her head bumped into her gravestone. It didn't hurt. It felt like a soft pillow instead of the cold, unforgiving granite that it was.

Inch by inch, her head slid down the front of her gravestone as her failing eyes saw the ground coming closer . . . closer . . . closer . . .

CHAPTER TWO

Wednesday, 11:14 p.m.

*G*inger began to regain consciousness. She was lying on her back and could feel her head throbbing, but otherwise, her senses were dull. She felt like she'd been asleep for three days, then awakened in the middle of the night. The room was completely black. Her body shivered. Why was the house so cold?

Her hands began to regain their sense of touch, but instead of feeling the smooth, warm sheets of her bed, she felt the cold, damp . . . grass? Ginger wiggled her toes and realized she was wearing shoes. She began to touch herself all over. She was fully dressed and wearing an apron.

Where was she, and how the heck did she get there?

Ginger located her cell phone in her apron pocket, took it out, woke it up, and held it over her face. It was eleven-fourteen p.m. She turned on her flashlight app and projected the beam in one direction and then another. She saw trees and bushes. Gravestones.

She was in the cemetery. Why in the world was she sleeping in the cemetery? Nothing made sense.

Memories flashed by like headlights on a busy freeway. She concentrated to try to slow them down, but they were disjointed, sketchy, and out of order. It was like trying to recall an old, half-forgotten dream. She remembered a man talking to her about a reverse mortgage. No, wait—that was a TV commercial.

Ginger tried to sit up, got dizzy, and quickly turned to the side and vomited. She eased herself back into her original position, flat on her back, to let her stomach settle.

She called 9-1-1.

"Ginger? What's the matter, sugarplum?"

"Sherry, I'm in the cemetery, and I don't know how I got here." Ginger was heartened to realize that at least she'd remembered Sherry's name.

"Old Coreyville Cemetery, behind your house? So, you got yourself all disoriented and went wandering around out there in the dark, not knowing why you were there?"

"No, it's not like that, Sherry. I'm on the ground. I just woke up and I can't remember much, but my head is throbbing like crazy. I think somebody attacked me. I need an ambulance."

"Okay, sugarplum. Just stay put, and I'll get you some help right away. And don't hang up."

"I won't." Ginger could hear Sherry radioing the paramedics.

Sherry came back to the phone. "So, did you have anything to drink tonight, or maybe take some pain pills?"

"Now, you know I don't drink," Ginger said. "Do I? I'm pretty sure I don't. My memories are all jumbled up."

"Well, I've never seen you take a drink, but honey, working this job, you learn that a lot of folks do their drinking in private. Lord, you'd be shocked to know how many times I get calls from them people. One night, a certain somebody—I can't say who—was having some fun with her new margarita machine and got falling-down drunk—literally. She fell off her back porch and landed in the dang flowerbed, face first. Nearly suffocated. She like to have never got all that crap out of her nose. Her yard people had just added new mulch, and you know how godawful it smells."

Ginger suddenly realized that she couldn't smell anything —not the grass, not the honeysuckle, not even the vomit she'd spewed onto the ground right beside her.

She smelled NOTHING.

She licked her arm and tasted NOTHING.

"Ginger? Are you still there?"

Under her breath, she said, "I can't smell or taste anything."

"What?"

"Wait—I just remembered something. I was in my kitchen, working on a cake recipe, and somebody called me on the phone—Susanna Clampford, I think—but after that, it's fuzzy."

Ginger saw a powerful light approaching her.

"They're here, Sherry. I'm hanging up now. Thanks so much."

"Any time, sugarplum."

The man behind the flashlight had a gravelly sounding voice. "Ginger?"

It was Boot Hornamer, the eighty-something-year-old Justice of the Peace. He must have been driving around and heard the call for the ambulance on his radio.

"Boot, what are you doing out and about this time of night?" But she already knew the answer. He was nocturnal to hear him tell it, sleeping maybe two to three hours a day, usually in the afternoon.

He was chomping on a big wad of chewing tobacco, as usual. "Paramedics will be here shortly, Ginger. How bad are you hurting?"

"My head's killing me, but otherwise, I think I'm okay."

"What are you doing out here at this time of night, girl?" He spit tobacco juice into a bush.

"I don't know. I'm having trouble remembering."

He leaned down with his powerful flashlight, blinding her. "Looks like you're bleeding."

"I am?"

"Yeah, you've got blood on your hands." He inspected each hand. "But I don't see any cuts."

"Really?" She held her hands up to her eyes. In the bright light from Boot's flashlight, she could see the dried blood.

"You said you've got a headache. Maybe the blood's from your head." He knelt beside her and inspected her head, digging into her scalp with his fingers. "Does this hurt?"

"Ow! You're pulling my hair!"

"Sorry. Your head ain't bleeding, as far as I can tell."

"Well, that's good to know. Thanks."

"You feel like trying to get up?"

"No. I think I'd better wait for the paramedics."

"Yeah, that's probably a good idea." He stood up. "You know, when I was walking up, I heard you telling Sherry that somebody called you on the phone and that's why you came out here."

"Yeah, I think that's what happened. I mean, I must have had some reason to come out here at night. I think Susanna Clampford called me from the cemetery, and I came out her to meet her for some reason. I can't remember exactly why, though."

"Wait. You just said something new."

"I did?"

"Yeah. You said she called you from the cemetery."

"Yeah, I did say that, but I'm not sure if it really happened."

"Susanna Clampford's the one who owns that big bakery in Marshall, right? Your number-one enemy?"

"I don't have any enemies, Boot. Not really."

He spit to the side.

"If my head's not bleeding," she held up her hands, "then where did this blood come from?"

"Good question." He inspected the area. "There's a shovel over here. Looks like blood on the handle. Hey, this is your shovel, Ginger."

"What? No, it couldn't be mine."

"It's got your name on it."

"Well, I can't imagine why I would have been walking around out here at night with a shovel. It doesn't make any sense."

The paramedics arrived and began to check her out.

Boot continued to nose around with his flashlight for a while and then came back to Ginger. "There's a body over there."

"A body?" Ginger's mind raced as she tried to jog her memory.

"Just a few yards up the trail. It's a woman. Looks like somebody bashed her head in."

"Oh, God. She's dead? Did you recognize her?"

"Well, her face has got blood all over it, so I'm not sure, but it looks like it might be Susanna Clampford."

"No."

"I didn't really know her, but I've seen her around."

"Oh, God."

"And, uh, it looks like the murder weapon is your shovel."

"Oh, no. I don't understand what happened, Boot."

The paramedics transferred Ginger to a stretcher.

Boot said, "I gotta call the chief, Ginger, so don't be surprised when he shows up at the hospital asking all kinds of questions."

"But, you don't think that I—"

"It don't matter what I think. Somebody killed that poor woman, and I gotta do my job." He took out his phone.

The paramedics picked up the stretcher and carried her out of the cemetery.

Ginger tried to focus all her brain power on remembering what had happened. She pictured Susanna standing over her with a shovel and swinging it at her. Then she got up and fought with Susanna.

Did that really happen?

And did she then grab the shovel away from Susanna and start beating her with it?

She couldn't imagine herself doing that, but if Susanna attacked her with a shovel, maybe Ginger's old hatred for the woman had come flooding back and caused her to go after Susanna with a blind vengeance.

She prayed that wasn't true.

CHAPTER THREE

Wednesday, 11:47 p.m.

Coreyville Hotel was a stately five-story building that was built in 1952, located on town square across from the courthouse. The first floor was occupied by the lobby, a large restaurant, a bar, and two conference halls.

The hotel had nearly gone out of business three times, had been renovated twice, and had received a major facelift in 2008. Occupancy rates were rarely high except during the annual two-week carnival. The hotel was currently at full capacity.

Al Fenster, sixty-seven, was sitting in the hotel barroom with his large belly pressed tightly against the edge of the bar, making it physically impossible for him to fall off his stool if he happened to get drunk and pass out. He almost chuckled thinking about it. At least there was one advantage to his obesity.

He gazed up at the screen's flashing bright colors, fully

aware that his shiny dome was partially obstructing the view of the men sitting at the table behind him watching Sports Center.

He was there first. Let them move to another table. Al did whatever he wanted, without apology.

A young bartender named Billy delivered another White Russian. "This one's got a little more vodka, sir. I think you'll like it better."

"Billy, I've been sitting here for hours, and I'm gonna come back tomorrow night and the next night, so don't you think it's about time we put ourselves on a first-name basis?"

"Whatever you like, sir."

"Well, what I'd like is for you to start calling me Al."

"Yes, sir, Al. Are you in town for the carnival?"

"I'm not a sideshow, if that's what you think."

"Oh, no, sir—I mean, Al. I didn't mean that."

Al laughed. "Don't get excited, man. I probably would make a pretty good sideshow." He raised his voice. "Step right up, folks, and direct your attention to the amazing Al. He's got the world's biggest belly."

One of the men at the table behind him said, "Hey, dude, hold it down. We're trying to hear the show."

Al waved him off.

"Sorry," Billy said. "I didn't mean to offend you."

"Aw, you can't offend me. But maybe this will give you a laugh: I'm a contestant in Ginger Lightley's Bake-Off."

"Oh, really?"

"Surprised?"

"Well, I just thought you—"

"You thought I was here to eat the cakes, not bake them, right?" Al patted his stomach.

Billy snickered, then looked embarrassed.

Al enjoyed embarrassing people.

Billy said, "No . . . I thought you might be one of the judges."

"Nope, I'm the proud owner and operator of Al's Deli and Bakery in Longview."

"I've heard of that."

"So, you're probably wondering why I'm staying here at the hotel. Well, I'll tell you why, Billy, my man. It's because there's no way I'm making that twenty-minute drive home after all this booze."

"That's smart, Al. Very responsible of you."

"Yeah, but that's not the real reason. I booked a room for three nights like all the other knuckleheads in Ginger's rigged contest."

"Well, if you think it's rigged, then why bother with it?"

"Okay, fair enough. You got me. It's probably not rigged, but sometimes it sure seems like it when Ginger walks off with the first-prize trophy every year."

"I love Ginger's little coffee cakes."

Al was beginning to slur. "Sure, they're great. But mine are the greater-est, and I'm gonna win first prize. I guarantee it." He knew he'd just said something that didn't sound quite right, but so what? At least he wasn't slurring his words like some drunk.

"You guarantee it, huh?"

"You don't believe me? You think it's the liquor talking, don't you?"

Billy shrugged. "Well, you did just say that your cakes are the 'greater-est.' That's not really a word, Al."

Al sat up straight. "Are you an English teacher, Billy? It

that what you are? No, you mark my words: Ginger Lightley will not win that first-prize trophy this year because that baby's going back to Longview in the passenger seat of my Toronado."

"What's a Toronado?"

Al was incensed. "What's a Toronado? It's a fine luxury car, boy. An Oldsmobile."

Billy had a blank look on his face.

Al shook his head. "Oh, just forget it."

A man from the end of the bar said, "Hey, bartender, can I get some service down here?"

Billy walked over to the man.

Al checked his watch. The bar was open until two a.m., so he had another two hours to drink. He enjoyed drinking—especially with a friend—but his drinking buddy, the thirty-six-year-old Bobby Boudreaux, turned out to be a lightweight. It wasn't long before he'd gotten drunk and angry, and then stormed out.

Bobby owned Doggers in Gladewater, a gourmet hot dog restaurant and bakery. Who'd ever heard of such a thing? Still, he was a good-natured old boy, and fun to hang out with until he got drunk. They had two things in common: a love for baking and a burning desire to beat Ginger Lightley at her own game.

But as much as Al enjoyed bragging about his baking abilities, his girlfriend, Maybelle Rogers—owner of Maybelle's Bakery in Tyler—was the one who had a real shot at dethroning Ginger. Al was a hack and he knew it—like an auto mechanic pretending to be a French pastry chef. His forte was the deli. Meats and cheeses. His bakery items were nothing special, and he wouldn't have even signed up for the bake-off if Maybelle hadn't been participating.

Maybelle was a successful businesswoman. Al was a terrible money manager and was about to go bankrupt. But together, they could become the king and queen of East Texas sweets and meats —as long as Maybelle's daughter Caroline didn't get in the way.

Caroline said folks in their sixties were too old for romance, but Al knew better, and he was gunning for the perfect marriage of sex and money.

He noticed that Billy was having a private conversation on his cell phone. That was something Al would never tolerate from his own employees.

Billy put his phone away and walked over to him. "Well, Al, as of tonight, you've got one less competitor."

"What are you talking about?"

"My buddy's a paramedic. The owner of that bakery in Marshall—Susanna something—she's dead."

Al tried not to let the satisfaction show on his face. "What happened to her?"

"Somebody beat her in the head with a shovel—right out there in Old Coreyville Cemetery. Ginger Lightley was out there too. She's in the emergency room."

"Oh, no."

"Yeah. She's a nice lady. Everybody loves her. I hope she's gonna be okay." Billy walked away.

Al quickly took out his phone and texted Maybelle: *Can I come to your room? It's important.*

She answered immediately: *Sure.*

Al left the bar, went into the men's restroom off the lobby, took out a travel-size bottle of Scope, poured the contents into his mouth and gargled with it, and threw the empty bottle in the trash. Then he took the elevator up to the third floor, where Ginger had booked rooms for all of her contestants. He went to Maybelle's door and tapped lightly.

She let him in. "It's nearly midnight, Al. It's way past my bedtime."

He slurred. "Sorry. I woke you up with my text?"

"No. I wasn't sleeping." She smiled. "I was lying in bed thinking about you."

He grinned. "You were?"

"Well, sure." She stepped in close and looked up into his eyes. "And you know what was going through my head while I was lying in bed thinking about you?" She put her hand on his chest.

"Uh . . ."

She stepped back and gave him a stern look. "Al, you've been smoking those stinky cigars again. I can smell it all over you."

"No, babe, it's not me. It was a guy in the bar."

"They let them smoke cigars in the bar? Yuck."

"Yeah, I know. Ever since I quit, they smell nasty to me too."

She cocked her head to one side. "How many drinks have you had?"

"I don't know. A few."

"I'll try to breathe through my mouth." She moved in close. "Now, where was I? Oh, yeah. See if you can guess what I'm thinking right now." She began to unbutton his shirt.

"Wait, wait, Maybelle. I hate to stop you, believe me—more than anything in the world—but I've got to tell you something."

"What is it?"

"Susanna Clampford is dead."

"Dead? What happened to her?"

"She was murdered in the cemetery," he said. "Somebody beat her in the head with a shovel."

"Are you kidding me? She was killed in the cemetery with a shovel? You don't think that somebody actually—"

"Carried out the plan?"

"Al, this is bad. I mean, of course it's bad. It's terrible—horrific that she was murdered—but what if the police think we were involved? I've been right here in my room since nine o'clock, but nobody's been here with me, so I guess, technically, I don't have an alibi. How about you?"

He hesitated, apparently a split-second too long.

She blurted, "Oh, Al, you didn't have anything to do with it, did you?"

"No, of course not. I can't believe you even have to ask."

"I'm sorry, but . . ."

"Maybe we don't belong together after all." Was he drunk out of his mind? What was he doing, telling her that? What was he gonna say if she agreed with him? He was a complete idiot for sticking his neck out so far, but the words were already out there, hanging in the air, and the longer she took to respond, the more likely that he'd just blown it.

She said, "Don't say that, baby. I trust you."

"I know you do. I don't know why I said that. Oh, and there's more news."

"Oh, God. What?"

"Ginger Lightley's in the hospital."

"What happened to her?"

"I don't know, but she was in the cemetery too."

"Oh, my. It was all in the plan. How badly is she hurt?"

"I don't know."

"Should we go down to the hospital and check on her, see how she's doing?"

"Well, it's a nice thought," he said.

"But at this time of night?"

"You're the one who suggested it."

"Yes, but, you know, we could have already been asleep when the word went out," she said. "No, we'll go see her tomorrow if she's still in the hospital."

"That'll work."

"I mean, we could run down there and make a big show of it, but personally, I'd prefer to spend the evening with you." She gave him a long, passionate kiss on the lips.

"You don't feel just a little bit guilty?"

Maybelle raised her eyebrows and smiled. "Not yet." She removed his belt.

"But what if we get caught? Caroline's right down the hallway."

"No, she's not. You worry too much, Al. She just called me a few minutes ago to say she was leaving the bakery."

"She was still at the bakery? It's midnight. Sounds to me like she's finally got herself a boyfriend."

"I wish. But no, she's just a workaholic. Anyway, she won't be here until after one, so I told her not to bother me when she gets in. Now, where were we?"

CHAPTER FOUR

Thursday, 12:25 a.m.

The radiology technician rolled Ginger's wheelchair into her ER room. Her boyfriend, Reverend Elijah Bideman, was sitting in the room waiting for her. As pastor of Corey Acres Baptist Church, Elijah made trips to the hospital several times per week, visiting the sick and comforting family members, but it was the first time he'd ever needed to be there for her.

He stood up. "How are you feeling, sweetie?"

She suddenly realized that her mascara was surely smeared into raccoon eyes and that her lipstick was long gone. Elijah had never seen her face looking like this, and she had hoped he wouldn't until after they were married—assuming he ever popped the question.

"Oh, Elijah, I'm sorry to get you up in the middle of the night. Yeah, I'm okay, I think. We'll see, I guess. They just ran a CT Scan on my head."

The tech helped Ginger onto her bed and then rolled the wheelchair out of the room.

"They think you might have brain damage?" he asked.

"No, no, the doctor doesn't really think so, but he says it's standard practice to do the scan in cases like mine. I lost some of my short-term memory, but it seems to be coming back pretty quickly. What worries me more is that I can't smell or taste anything. It's driving me crazy. But the doctor thinks I'll be completely back to normal in a few days since I was only unconscious for five minutes or so."

"How do you know how long you were unconscious?"

"Well, because I checked my phone. Susanna called me at 10:55, and when I woke up in the cemetery, it was 11:07, so when you add in some time for me to walk out there . . . anyway, the doc says that means I've probably only suffered a mild trauma. So, if the CT Scan looks good, he might send me home tonight."

"Really? Seems like you should be admitted for a couple of days so they can monitor you in case you start having problems."

"Oh, you know how it is now with the insurance companies these days. You come in to have a baby, and they rush you in and out so fast—it's almost like curb service. And I'm on Medicare, so they're sure not gonna keep me for long. But don't worry. Jane's coming to pick me up. I'll stay with the girls until I'm better."

Ginger's best friends—Jane Appletree, Barb Omatta, and Ethel Eggly, who she liked to call the girls—were also her business partners as co-owners of Ginger Bread House, a bed and breakfast on the outskirts of town.

"Well, that's great, but how are they going to keep an eye on you while they're busy running the business?"

"I appreciate your concern, sweetie. I really do. But the girls will take care of me. Besides, I may be completely back to normal by tomorrow." She offered an optimistic grin.

Elijah stepped in close to her bed, leaned down, and kissed her on the check. "So, how did this happen?"

She sighed. "It was the craziest thing. I was in the kitchen testing recipes and talking to Fredrick and—"

"Who's Fredrick?"

"One of my bake-off people, Fredrick Marcello. He owns a bakery in Longview: Frosted by Fredrick. Anyway, he had come by to chat about baking."

"Wasn't it awfully late for him to be dropping in? What time did he come?"

"Around ten. Oh, and he was going on and on about Kate."

"Who's Kate?"

"Kate Lake. She used to work in his bakery, but a few months ago, she broke up with him and opened her own bakery. It really hurt him. But the crazy thing is that, apparently, he's the one who gave her the startup money. And it would have taken at least ten thousand dollars—bare minimum. I guess he thought he could buy her back."

"Love can make you do crazy things," he said.

"Anyway, she's in town too, for the contest."

"It's like a soap opera."

"Yeah, it is. But anyway, we mostly talked about our baking philosophies, so I didn't mind. It was interesting. The look and taste of the frosting are the most important things to him. I disagreed, of course, since I don't put frosting on anything.

But he made some good points, and he's a sharp, energetic young man, so I understand why his business is doing well."

"Seems like your memory's just fine."

"It is—for everything that happened up until I went into the cemetery. After that, things are still a little fuzzy."

"Do you remember why you went out there?"

"I got a call from Susanna Clampford right after Fredrick left."

"She's the one who was murdered."

"Yes. She said she needed to talk to me. It was urgent, and she was on her way to my house through the cemetery. Then it sounded like she dropped her phone, and—"

"You went out to check on her."

"Yeah."

He shook his head. "You should have called me, sweetie. But why in the world would she take that shortcut through the cemetery at eleven o'clock at night?"

"You've got me. Six years ago when Lester died, she came to the funeral, and she was out there for the graveside service, so I guess that's how she knew about the shortcut."

"Still, it doesn't make sense," he said. "Why not just drive over or take the long way around on the sidewalk? It's not that much farther."

"I don't know."

"I just wish you'd called me instead of going out there in the dark by yourself. Or called 9-1-1. Why didn't you just call the police?"

"Because . . . I don't know. I had a flashlight. And besides, I know that place like the back of my hand."

"I know you like to stop at Lester's grave and chat."

She studied his face. "Does that upset you?"

"No, not at all."

"So, where was I . . . oh, yeah. I followed the trail and it was windy out there. And my flashlight batteries started dying, and—"

"You should have turned back."

"So, when I got to my gravestone—"

"Your gravestone? You mean Lester's?"

"Mine's right next to his."

"Of course, that's right. I knew that."

"Because, you know, we thought we'd live a long life and die around the same time. I guess most couples think that."

"Sure."

"But somebody added a date of death to my gravestone."

"What?"

"Yeah. It really freaked me out. And the date was today—actually yesterday, since it's after midnight."

"You're kidding."

"No, I'm not. Go out there and look for yourself if you don't believe me."

"I believe you. It's just that . . . you said you're having problems with memory."

"I am, but it's starting to come back. I just remembered that part a few minutes ago, in the middle of my CT Scan."

Elijah nodded. He looked like he was trying to believe her.

"Of course, I can't be sure," she said. "Maybe my brain's playing tricks on me, but that's what I remember. I was bent over, looking at my gravestone when somebody hit me on the head with something—probably my own shovel—and I passed out."

"Your own shovel?"

The door opened and Chief of Police Daniel Foenapper

stepped in. He was a young Barney Fife—slightly more competent, but certainly no Andy. "How are you doing, Ginger?"

She appreciated his words of concern, but they didn't match the look on his face. Still, she had to answer. "Pretty good, considering."

"Hello, Pastor."

Elijah nodded. "Chief."

The chief studied Elijah's face. "I imagine you'll be getting a few calls in the morning, Elijah, after the good people of Coreyville find out what happened tonight in their little innocent town. That poor woman viciously murdered. Ginger brutally attacked. Doesn't happen very often around here."

"You do an excellent job of keeping us safe, Chief," Elijah said.

Ginger nearly gagged. She knew Elijah was just being diplomatic, but that was over the top.

"Well, thanks, Pastor. Nobody cares more about the people of this town than me. Well, except maybe you, of course." He chuckled.

Ginger said, "I was just telling Elijah about the date of death that somebody carved into my gravestone. Did you see it?"

The chief looked dumbfounded. "What are you talking about, Ginger?"

"In the cemetery, on my gravestone—didn't you see it?"

"Yes, I saw your gravestone. We walked the entire area very carefully, picking up evidence and taking photos, and I can assure you that there is no date of death on your gravestone."

"How can you be so sure?"

"Because when I noticed the date of birth on your gravestone, I was surprised. I figured you to be a few years younger than that. So, I definitely would have noticed if there had been a date of death on there."

"But I know I saw it. Somebody had carved it right into the stone, and it was today's date—like they were planning to kill me today. And they almost did."

The chief said, "I'm sorry, Ginger, really, but—"

"I remember it so clearly," she said.

Elijah said, "But, honey—"

"Yes, I know. My head's not quite back to normal."

The chief said, "I'm sorry you were attacked."

Elijah looked at the chief. "Any idea who might have done it?"

"Not a clue at this point, but we'll track them down, that's for sure."

"What about Susanna?" Ginger asked. "Did you find any evidence to help you identify the killer?"

"Yes, and we sent it to the lab. But I can tell you this much right now: whoever killed that woman must have really hated her."

"So, you think it was a crime of passion," Elijah said.

"Definitely. Her face was so messed up—her own mother wouldn't recognize her."

"Chief, please," Ginger said, "you don't have to be so graphic."

"I'm just saying that somebody really went after her with that shovel. Your shovel."

"Well, I don't understand how my shovel got out there in the cemetery. It should have been in my tool shed. Wait—I know who attacked me. All of a sudden, I remember."

The chief and Elijah said, "Who?"

"It was Susanna."

"The dead woman?" the chief asked. "And you just now remembered that?"

"I was bent over, looking at my gravestone when I heard something behind me and looked back. It was Susanna, about to swing the shovel at my head."

"You're sure?" the chief asked.

"Pretty sure," she said.

The chief said, "Hmm. You and Susanna Clampford have been fighting for years, haven't you?"

"No, we haven't been fighting. That's ridiculous. Who told you that?"

"Seems to be common knowledge," the chief said.

"I wouldn't put much stock in rumors, Chief," Elijah said.

"Well, there is some truth to it," she said. "I mean, we were never friends, but things never got physical between us."

"I understand the friction between you two goes way back," the chief said.

Ginger said, "Elijah, Jane's on her way up. Why don't you go on home and get some sleep? I'll be fine."

"That's okay. I'd rather stay for a while," he said.

The chief went on. "From what I hear, back when you and Susanna were in college, you stole her boyfriend."

"Well, that's just not true," she said. "I mean . . . that's not exactly what happened."

"Oh, but I think it is," the chief said. "Susanna was dating Lester Lightley when you decided you wanted him for yourself."

"Easy, Chief," Elijah said.

The chief continued. "Isn't it true that you were determined to steal Lester away from her, and that you wanted him so bad that you slept with him?"

Ginger sat up straight in the bed. "Who told you that?"

Elijah raised his voice. "Chief, you are way out of line."

The chief went on. "And isn't that why Susanna has always hated you?"

"That's not what happened," she said.

"You didn't sleep with him while Susanna was still dating him?" the chief asked.

"Daniel, you're about to have to haul me off to jail," Elijah said, "because I'm about to punch you in the nose."

"No. Stop, Elijah. Don't hit him," Ginger said. "It's true. I'm ashamed of it, but yes, it's true. I was a foolish young woman, and I was just lucky that things worked with Lester."

The chief said, "So, is that why you got into a big fight with Susanna in the cemetery? Did she insult you? Did she call you names and make you so mad that you hit her over the head with your shovel again and again until she was dead?"

"No!" Ginger said.

Elijah shouted, "Chief!"

"And that's why there was blood on the shovel and on your hands. You killed her, didn't you?"

"No! I did not kill her!"

Elijah got in his face. "Chief, you need to go!" He pointed to the door.

The chief held up his hands. "Okay, okay. I'm leaving. But we're gonna talk more in the morning." He backed toward the door. "I apologize. Feel better. Sorry, Pastor. Just doing my job. Goodnight."

After a few moments of awkward silence, Elijah said, "Well, that's a story I've never heard before."

"I'm sorry. I should have told you. Are you angry with me? I wouldn't blame you."

"No. I'm not angry."

He was a terrible liar. Being a man of God, he didn't get much practice.

Jane Appletree peeked in, smiling. "Your taxi has arrived."

"Jane, come in," Ginger said.

"Hey, Elijah."

"Hello, Jane."

"Okay, girl, you ready to go?" Jane asked.

"No, not yet. I'm not even sure the doctor's gonna release me, but I'm hoping."

"No problem," Jane said. "I'm just glad you're okay. You are okay, right?"

Ginger glanced at Elijah. "Yeah. I think so. We'll see."

"I'm gonna go, Ginger," Elijah said with a stern expression.

"Okay. Thanks for coming. Get some rest, sweetie."

He went out the door.

Jane looked confused and concerned. "What just happened here?"

Ginger shook her head. "Something even worse than getting hit in the head with a shovel."

CHAPTER FIVE

Thursday, 1:07 a.m.

Chief Foenapper marched into Coreyville Hotel with two of his deputies. He questioned the desk clerk and learned that Susanna Clampford and Marilyn Monastrovi were registered in Room 309. The chief wondered why Ms. Monastrovi had not gone out looking for her missing roommate. If she wasn't in her room, and they couldn't locate her, she would become a suspect.

They took the elevator up to the third floor and went to the room. The chief banged on the door. If he woke up some of the other guests, so be it. This was important police business. Exciting business. The kind that didn't come to Coreyville very often. He was an early-to-bed, early-to-rise kind of man, usually sound asleep at one o'clock in the morning. This was the exception. This was the kind of police work he lived for.

A woman peeked out the door. She spoke in a soft, syrupy-

Southern, almost-seductive voice. "What's the matter, officer?"

"Are you Marilyn Monastrovi?"

"Yes."

She was average height, slim, but shapely. Looked like she'd been sleeping. There was no makeup on her face, and her long brown hair was wild and tangled, like she'd been riding a motorcycle without a helmet. She was maybe forty, a good ten years older than him, and her long nightgown looked like one of his mother's, yet there was something about her that almost made him forget why he was there.

"I'm Coreyville Police Chief Daniel Foenapper, ma'am."

"What's this about, Daniel?"

When he was on the job, he insisted that everyone call him chief, but he loved her breathy voice and the way his name floated across her tongue and out between her full lips.

"Mind if I come in, Ms. Monastrovi?"

She opened the door.

He told his deputies to wait in the hallway, and he went inside and closed the door. The only light in the room was coming from a lamp. He flipped on the overhead lights.

"You should probably sit down, ma'am."

"Please call me Marilyn."

He noticed that the bed closest to the door looked slept in, while the other one was still made up.

She turned to see what he was looking at. "Susanna."

"Really, Marilyn, I think you'd better sit down."

She sat on the side of her bed. "Did something happen to Susanna? I was reading a book and must have dozed off."

"There's no easy way to say this."

"No, please . . ."

"I'm sorry, but Susanna is dead."

"Oh, my God. Oh, my God."

"She was murdered."

"Murdered?" The tears began to flow. "I don't understand. How could this happen?"

"I'll tell you the details in just a minute. First, I need to ask you a few questions. I'm sorry, but I really have to do it this way." He took out his small spiral notebook. "When was the last time you saw Susanna?"

"Right before I went out to the car."

"What time was that?"

"Probably around nine-thirty."

He recorded it in his notebook. "And when did you come back up to the room?"

"A little after eleven, I think."

"What were you doing for all that time?"

"Sitting in the car, playing a game on my phone."

"For an hour and a half?"

"I'm really hooked on this new one I downloaded. I know, it sounds silly. I shouldn't be wasting so much time on games, but the truth is that sometimes Susanna gets on my—got on my nerves. Oh, no. Is this my fault? I shouldn't have left her alone."

"No, I'm sure it wasn't your fault. So, when you came back up to the room, Susanna was gone?"

"Yes. But she left me a note." Marilyn got up and went to the dresser, picked it up, and gave it to him.

He read it out loud. "Walking over to Ginger's house. Don't wait up." He looked up at Marilyn. "What do you think this was about? I mean, what could have been so important that she had to meet with Ginger so late at night?"

"I don't know."

"You think it had anything to do with their long-running feud?"

Marilyn hesitated. "You knew about that?"

"Word gets around."

"Susanna hated Ginger."

"And what about Ginger? Did she hate Susanna?"

"I don't know. Probably. But they were always civil—at least when I saw them together. So, exactly what happened to Susanna?"

"It's graphic."

She cringed. "Tell me anyway. Otherwise, I'll be imagining something even worse."

"We found her body in the cemetery."

"The cemetery? What was she doing in the cemetery?"

"Taking the shortcut to Ginger's house, according to Ginger, but along the way somebody attacked her and beat her head in with a shovel."

"Oh, God, who would do such a thing? And why?"

"That's what I'm working on."

"Of course. Excuse me." She went into the bathroom and came back with a box of tissues. She took one out and wiped her eyes. "So, you think Ginger did this to Susanna?"

He shrugged. "It's possible, but I'm just beginning my investigation."

"This is awful."

"Ginger's in the ER."

"What happened to her?"

"She thinks Susanna hit her over the head with a shovel."

"No. Really? Do you believe that?"

"I don't know, and Ginger's not even sure about it.

The doctor thinks she's gonna be okay, but she got a concussion, and she's not sure exactly what happened out there. What do you think? Was Susanna capable of violence?"

"I don't know what to believe. It's all just crazy."

"So, what was your relationship with Susanna?"

"I manage her bakery. Been working for her since 1999."

"Wow, 1999. You must have been a kid."

She smiled. "Thanks. Actually, I was twenty-nine."

So, she was a little older than he'd guessed, but he still felt a strong urge to ask her for a date. Maybe he would, after the case was solved, assuming she wasn't the killer. Oh, please, don't let her be the killer.

"So, you and Susanna must have been close."

She wiped her nose. "She was like a mother to me."

"Did she have any enemies—other than Ginger?"

"No. I mean, I wouldn't call them enemies."

"Then what would you call them?"

Marilyn seemed to be searching for just the right words. "Let's just say that she wasn't very likable sometimes. It even took me quite a while to warm up to her. She could be so outgoing and funny, and everybody loved her laugh. It was infectious. But then she'd just turn on you—without warning—and make you feel like you were worthless. I talked to her about it many times, tried to make her understand how much she was hurting people."

"But she just kept doing it."

"Yeah," she said. "She didn't have many friends other than me. And it was always hard to keep employees."

"Sounds like there could be a long list of people who might have wanted to kill her."

"I didn't say that. Just because somebody treats you like dirt, it doesn't automatically turn you into a murderer."

"True, but what about Ginger Lightley? You think she's capable of murder?"

"Oh, I doubt it. But who knows. They were fierce rivals. Susanna called Ginger her nemesis."

"Oh, really?"

"But I don't know if Ginger thought of Susanna that way."

"Okay." He closed his notebook and put it in his pocket. "Thank you, Marilyn. You've been very helpful."

"You're welcome, Daniel."

"I may have some more questions for you in the next few days."

"Well, we were supposed to be here through Saturday—you know, for the cake judging at the carnival. But now . . ."

"I understand," he said. "Well, if I do have any more questions I'll give you a call. What's your phone number?"

She gave him her work and cell numbers.

"Look, I know this is tough for you, but I need to have my men come in and collect all of Susanna's property. Her suitcase, clothes, makeup, and everything else."

"Whatever you need, Daniel. It's not like I'll be able to go back to sleep anyway."

CHAPTER SIX

Thursday, 1:32 a.m.

Twenty-eight-year-old Fredrick Marcello was in his hotel room, fidgeting in a leather arm chair like a young schoolgirl. He was two doors down from his ex-girlfriend, Kate Lake. Marilyn Monastrovi's room was between them.

Fredrick was constantly thinking, planning, and worrying —which may have been what kept him thin because he never exercised, and he ate anything he wanted. He sought perfection in everything—particularly when it came to baking and his unique frosting creations. He'd been mulling over ideas for improving his fresh peach frosting when he overheard the police chief in Marilyn's room.

Once the chief and his deputies were gone, Fredrick got up, peeked out his door to make sure the coast was clear, and tiptoed down to Kate's room. He loved her so much—she was the frosting on his cake—but he couldn't afford to let anyone see him associating with her. He knocked softly on her door.

He waited ten seconds and knocked again.

Kate opened the door in her robe and slippers, grabbed Fredrick by the waistband, yanked him inside, and shut the door. She hissed in a loud whisper, "What are you doing here? You're gonna ruin everything."

Kate Lake was twenty-two, five-foot-five, with the gravitas of a corporate CEO. The determined expression on her face, along with her spiked, fiery hair, said I'm running the show, so get out of my way. To Fredrick, it felt like she was the man in the relationship, but he didn't mind.

"I can't believe she's dead, Kate. Oh, I just can't believe it. Did you hear all that, through the wall? Oh, my goodness. I mean, I knew it was going to happen, but—"

"What are you talking about?"

"The plan. I'd forgotten about it, to be honest, but—"

"You're not making any sense," she said.

"When you called earlier and reminded me to stick with the plan, I went over to Ginger's house and stayed there talking to her until precisely ten-fifty-four, just like I was supposed to."

Kate's pale face turned whiter than a sheet. "Fredrick, when I told you to stick with the plan, I was talking about our plan—for us to stay away from each other and keep acting like we hated each other. That plan."

He flung his hand up to his mouth. "Oh. That plan."

"Look, if you had anything to do with what happened to Susanna Clampford, I do not want to know about it."

"No, of course I didn't."

"So, why are you here in my room?"

Fredrick grinned. "I just had to see you, baby."

She punched him in the chest. "You promised me you'd stay away from me. If anybody sees you going in or out of my room, it's all been for nothing. I'm screwed. But you don't care, do you?"

"Of course I care."

"Hey, if you can't learn to control your emotions, then we're done—for good."

"Aw, come on, Kate."

"No. I mean it. Our horrible public breakup was to make people feel sorry for me. It was a big fat lie, but it's working. My business is really starting to take off."

He pouted. "And I'm losing business since you left."

"Well, what does that tell you? But you can afford to lose a little business anyway. It's not gonna kill you."

"I know, but I miss you. I really, really miss you," he said. "But I want your bakery to be a success, so I'll keep letting people think I treated you like dirt."

"Then why are you here?"

"It's okay. Nobody saw me." He smiled. "And since I'm already here, how about we have a little us time?"

He reached for her, but she pushed him back.

"You're funny if you think I'm gonna reward you for doing the wrong thing," she said. "No, I'm gonna punish you."

He felt like a little boy who was about to be sent to the corner. "Punish me?"

She opened her robe and revealed her skimpy, red teddy.

His jaw dropped. "Looks like you were expecting me."

"No, I just like the way it makes my body feel: silky and sexy."

"Oh, baby." He stepped toward her.

She closed the robe and cinched it with dramatic flair. "You get nothing! And if you don't stick with our plan, you may never get anything ever again."

Fredrick held up his hands. "Okay, I'm sorry. You're right."

"Now, after I take home the first-prize trophy, maybe we can—"

"Whoa, whoa, whoa," he said. "I'm gonna win first prize."

"Because you have a better frosting than me? Nope. Not gonna happen."

"Wait—are you threatening me? Are you saying that if I don't let you win—"

"You're not gonna let me win. I'm gonna beat your butt, fair and square."

"Oh, you're on, missy. You actually think you can beat me? Hah."

"I know I can. Look, you make the best frosting in East Texas."

"Best in the country. In the world!"

"Yeah, maybe. But the contest is about the whole cake, and your frosting is a little better than mine, sure, but my cake will destroy yours."

"Oh, yeah?"

"Yeah." She got in his face. "My cake's gonna punch your little wimpy cake in the nose and flush it down the toilet."

"Well, well . . . we'll just see about that!"

She started laughing.

"What are you laughing at?"

"It's so easy to get you spun up."

He threw his head back. "Meany."

"Well, if I'm so mean, then why do you want to be with me, Fredrick?"

"Because . . . stop trying to confuse me."

"It's just so easy, I can't resist. Now, go back to your room and make sure nobody sees you."

"But what are we going to do if Ginger cancels the contest? Did you hear what the chief said? She's in the hospital. The whole thing's probably going to fall apart."

"Quit freaking out. The chief said she's gonna be okay. So, I doubt she'll cancel. She's too much of a competitor."

"I hope you're right."

"Now get back to your room and stay away from me. We hate each other. Remember?"

"Right. Got it."

CHAPTER SEVEN

Thursday, 2:00 a.m.

The emergency room doctor released Ginger, and Jane picked her up at the entrance. It would be a five-minute drive to Ginger Bread House.

"Thanks for coming to get me, Jane."

"No problem at all, sweetie. You know that."

"You suppose Barb and Ethel are still up?"

"Definitely. I got a text from Ethel a minute ago when I was walking out to get the car. I told her you'd just been released, and she said she'd have the hot cocoa waiting for us."

"Good. 'Cause I don't know if I can go to sleep right away. I may not sleep at all tonight."

"The pain meds aren't working?"

"It's not the pain. It's trying to figure out if it was really Susanna who hit me over the head and who killed her, and thinking about the look on Elijah's face when he found out that I slept with Lester in college, before we were married."

"Ginger, that was over forty years ago. You were just a young thing."

"I was old enough to know better. We just got carried away. I had no intention of going there, I can assure you."

"And you really think Elijah's gonna hold that against you?"

"Maybe."

"You don't seriously think he'd break up with you over that?"

"I don't know. I just don't know, Jane."

"He has to forgive you. He's a man of God. He preaches forgiveness. That's his thing."

"What if the church members find out?"

"I'm surprised they don't already know. I can't believe I didn't know. How did you keep it a secret for so long?"

"I just didn't tell anybody, and apparently, Susanna didn't either, but somebody found out and told the chief about it. Or maybe everybody knows and they've been talking behind my back for all these years."

"No. I can guarantee you that's not the case."

"Of course. What am I thinking? When you were running the café, you heard all the gossip."

"I'm surprised you never told me about it," Jane said. "I thought we shared everything."

"I'm sorry. I didn't tell you about it because I was trying to pretend it never happened, as though that would erase it from history."

"You'd need a time machine to do that."

"Oh, believe me, I wished I'd had one. But then I realized

that if I went back in time and changed that, Lester and I might never have fallen in love and gotten married."

"And he might have married Susanna instead."

"Oh, wow, and if he had, he probably would have died even younger. He would have been miserable with that woman. Oh, what am I saying? I shouldn't be talking about Susanna like that. She's dead."

"Lester never would have married her, Ginger. Come on."

"I don't know. You should have seen her back then. Tall, thin, gorgeous."

"You were beautiful too. You still are."

"I'm sure I look pretty awful right now."

After a few moments, Jane said, "You know, I hate to say it, but you're right to worry about the church members finding out, because the chief knows."

"Yeah, he's a blabbermouth."

"But even if the whole town finds out, Elijah's not gonna give up on you."

"He might lose his job, though. The deacons can't just stand by while their pastor's dating some Jezebel."

"Jezebel? Don't you think you're being a little melodramatic? Those deacons are not perfect. And as the Bible says, let he who hath not sinned cast the first stone."

"Well, sure, that's the way it should be, but you know that's not how it is."

"They'll make an exception for you. Especially if y'all get married."

"Elijah hasn't asked me to marry him."

"But it's only a matter of time, don't you think?"

"I'm not even sure I want to marry him."

"What? That's got to be the bump on your head talking.

You've been so excited about the prospect of spending the rest of your life with him. That's all you've been talking about—your second chance at love."

"But I just don't know if I can do it now. I mean, yeah, on the one hand, I would love to marry him, but on the other hand, I don't think I could ever be a pastor's wife."

"Because of sleeping with Lester before you got married?"

"I'm just not good enough, Jane. I realize that now. I'm not pure the way I need to be. And I don't think I ever could be."

"You're being too hard on yourself, sweetie. You see these pastors' wives running around all nice and cheery, and they seem like they're just perfect, but believe me, they're not. They've got some dirty little secrets hidden away somewhere. They're human like the rest of us."

"Maybe so, but I just don't think it'll work for me."

"Well, if Elijah loves you half as much as I think he does, he'll change your mind about that."

"No . . . I think we're probably done. Maybe it's just as well."

"Oh, quit feeling sorry for yourself."

"Why shouldn't I feel sorry for myself? Somebody tried to kill me tonight. And I could have permanent brain damage, for all I know."

"Not according to the ER doc. He said it was a minor concussion. That's all."

"So? What does he know? It's not his head."

"You know, maybe that bonk on the head did screw you up, because you sure don't sound like the Ginger I know."

"Yeah, well I'm not the Ginger I know either, to the best of my memory—which is not working very well. But, honestly, the thing that's bothering me even more than the loss of my short-term memory is that I've lost my sense of smell and taste. It makes me feel like I'm half dead."

"It's gonna be okay, Ginger. The doctor said you'd probably get over that in a couple of days."

"I sure hope so because my smelling and tasting abilities are what make me special. You know that, Jane. Without them . . . I'll never be able to create another cake recipe. Ever."

"You know what you need?"

"A miracle."

"No. You need a big mug of Ethel's hot cocoa, followed by a long night's sleep. And that's exactly what you're gonna get."

CHAPTER EIGHT

Thursday, 2:13 a.m.

*G*inger slept at home most nights, but on Tuesdays and Saturdays she did a sleepover with Jane, Barb, and Ethel at Ginger Bread House. Those nights were reserved for dominos, and had been for years, even before they purchased the grand old house, renovated it, and turned it into a lovely bed and breakfast. Ginger held a twenty-five percent stake and was involved in all business decisions, but the other three women lived there, drew salaries, and ran the place. It was a 24/7 job, and they loved it.

After a rocky start, Ginger Bread House had blossomed into a successful business venture, mostly because of its close association with Ginger's bakery. Guests knew they'd have access to an unlimited supply of Ginger's mini-loaf cakes during their stay. Plus, they might get a chance to visit with the famous Ginger Lightley when she dropped by.

Ginger didn't think of herself as famous, but many of the

guests did. They loved to hear about the history of Coreyville Coffee Cakes and how she came up with the idea for her various cake recipes, and Ginger loved talking about it.

When Ginger and Jane arrived, they went straight to the office as quietly as they could, mindful of their sleeping guests. It was a large room that had served as a library for the previous owner. There were desks with computers for conducting business, a round, wooden table for playing dominos, and a cozy spot near the front windows with four Queen Anne chairs surrounding a coffee table for the girls' late-night chats.

Barb and Ethel hurried over to them in their nightgowns and robes.

"Ginger, are you okay?" Barb asked.

"I'm fine."

Barb hugged her.

"We were worried to death about you, girl." Ethel gave her a hug.

"Yes, I imagine so," Ginger said. "It's not every day that one of your best friends nearly gets herself murdered."

"And in a cemetery, of all places," Barb said.

"Actually, I guess it's the ideal place," Ginger said. "I mean, everybody else out there is dead."

Ethel laughed.

"Well, at least you haven't lost your sense of humor," Barb said.

"Unfortunately, that may be the only thing I have left."

"What are you talking about?" Barb said. "You just said you were fine."

"She's been standing for too long," Jane said. "Let's go sit down."

They walked Ginger toward the sitting area.

"Have you got my cocoa ready, Ethel?" Ginger asked.

"Don't worry. It's on the coffee table waiting for you."

"Great," Ginger said. "But it's probably gonna taste like dirt."

Ethel looked at Jane. "Why's she being so mean?"

They sat down in their chairs.

"She's not being mean," Jane said.

"She always says she loves my cocoa," Ethel said. "Has she been lying to me all this time?"

"No, of course not," Jane said.

Ginger picked up her mug and tried to breathe in the aroma, and smelled . . . nothing. "You remembered the marshmallows, Ethel. Thank you." She took a sip but couldn't taste a thing. She frowned and shook her head.

Ethel looked at Jane. "I thought cocoa would make her feel better, but she hates it. I can see it on her face."

Jane tasted her cocoa. "There's nothing wrong with your cocoa, Ethel. It tastes great. The problem is with Ginger. She can't smell or taste anything."

"What are you talking about?" Barb said.

"The blow to Ginger's head gave her a mild concussion," Jane said. "She's lost her sense of smell and taste."

"You can't taste anything?" Ethel asked.

"But I'm sure it's only temporary," Barb said. "Right?"

"Yeah, according to the ER doctor," Ginger said. "My senses should come back within a few days."

"Oh, my goodness," Ethel said. "How are you gonna do your Sniff-Out at the contest on Saturday? Everybody loves that."

Ginger shrugged. The Sniff-Out was something Ginger

always did right before the announcement of the bake-off winners. She would hold up each cake entry, smell it, and name off at least two unusual ingredients she smelled in the cake. The carnival crowd always loved it. But she wouldn't be able to do it this year.

"When Jane called us, she said it was Susanna Clampford who attacked you in the cemetery," Barb said.

"That's right," Ginger said, "if my memory is correct."

"But then she ended up dead," Barb said. "I'm confused. Who killed her?"

"We don't know," Jane said. "But the chief says she was killed with Ginger's shovel."

Ethel nearly spilled her cocoa. "Ginger's shovel?"

"Yeah," Ginger said. "Apparently, somebody stole it out of my tool shed."

Jane said, "The chief has this theory that Susanna attacked Ginger, and then Ginger got into a tussle with her, took the shovel away, and killed her with it."

"Well, he's just crazy," Barb said. "But we already knew that."

Ethel said, "Did you tell him he was crazy, Ginger?"

"I wanted to," Ginger said. "But . . ."

Jane jumped in. "The blow to her head caused some memory loss."

"But it's temporary," Barb said, "right?"

"Probably," Jane said.

"But in the meantime," Barb said, "you can't tell the chief exactly what happened out there because you don't remember."

"It's not good," Ginger said.

"Well, it's just ridiculous," Ethel said. "The very idea that you could kill somebody. How could the chief think that?"

No one spoke for a few moments.

"I feel just awful about Susanna," Ginger said. "I couldn't stand that woman, but for her to be murdered . . . she didn't deserve that."

"No," Jane said, "she didn't."

A few moments passed as Ginger watched the girls sip their cocoa.

"The chief is a doggone idiot," Barb said.

"I can't really blame him for not believing me, because my memory's foggy. All I've got is bits and pieces. I remember a flashlight on the ground pointed at my gravestone, and the stone had my date of death carved into it, which completely freaked me out."

"It had your date of death on it?" Barb asked. "How did that get there?"

"Somebody carved it into the stone?" Ethel asked.

"Yes," Ginger said, "that's what I saw."

"That can't be right," Barb said. "You must have dreamed that after you got hit on the head."

"Maybe I did, because the chief says it's not on there. But I remember it so clearly."

"That's freaky, to know when you're gonna die," Ethel said. "What was the date?"

"Oh, don't be a ninny, Ethel," Barb said. "It was just a dream."

Ginger stared into space. "March 23, 2016."

"That's . . . that's today!" Ethel said. "Or yesterday, I mean. When did you see it? Was it before midnight?"

"Yes."

"So, it was like somebody planned to kill you last night," Ethel said, "and they wanted you to know you were about to die right before it happened. Creepy."

"But they didn't kill her," Jane said, "and it's not on the gravestone now."

"It's like magic," Ethel said. "Ginger was too strong to kill, so the date just vanished."

"You've been watching too many movies, Ethel," Barb said.

"I shouldn't have even told the chief about that," Ginger said. "It made him doubt everything else I said. And it really makes me look guilty since Susanna was killed with my shovel."

"Well, that's not your fault," Barb said.

"And her blood was on my hands," Ginger said. "At least they think it was her blood. The hospital took a sample of it at the chief's request, and the lab's going to test it."

"Oh, that'll really be bad if it was her blood on your hands," Ethel said. "How could that have happened?"

"As I said, the chief thinks that Susanna and I got into an argument that turned violent. That maybe she started hitting me, and I grabbed the shovel and hit her to protect myself. And then I guess he thinks I just went crazy with rage and beat her in the head until—"

"If you killed her, then who in the world knocked you out?" Barb said.

"Maybe he figures that after I killed her I was walking away, and I tripped and fell and hit my head on a gravestone or a rock."

"You don't really believe that's what happened," Jane said.

"I can't imagine that I would attack her," Ginger said. "I just wish I could remember."

"The chief's real good at making snap judgments," Barb said. "That's his specialty."

Ethel stared at Ginger. "Why are you wearing only one earring?"

Barb said, "Because she's trying to look like a pirate."

Ethel scrunched her nose. "Huh?"

"When I got to the hospital, the other one was missing," Ginger said, "and I'm really upset about it because they're the ones Lester gave me for my sixtieth birthday."

"Wasn't that just a few months before he died?" Barb asked.

"Yes," Ginger said.

Jane's cell phone rang, and she took it out of her pocket. "It's the chief. Probably for you." She handed her phone to Ginger.

"Hello, Chief. . . . Yeah, my phone's dead. . . . I don't know. I can't decide that right now. . . . Okay, I'll talk to you in the morning. Bye."

"What was that about?" Jane asked.

"He told me I should cancel the bake-off."

"He can't make you do that," Barb said. "You've got all these bakery owners in town and all the foodies and the other folks here for the carnival. Everybody looks forward to this. Doesn't he know what a big deal it is?"

"He doesn't care about any of that," Ginger said, "but he's probably right. I should cancel out of respect for Susanna. I still can't believe she's dead."

CHAPTER NINE

Thursday, 6:35 a.m.

Maybelle Rogers woke up to a text message alert. She read it and then tapped Al on the shoulder.

"Wake up, Al. I just got a text from Ginger. She sent it to all the contestants. She wants to meet with us this morning at eight-forty-five."

"Well, I guess that means she's out of the hospital."

"Yeah, but I'll bet she's going to cancel the bake-off."

Al sat up in bed. "No, no, she can't do that. You're gonna win first prize. Or if you don't, I will."

"Yeah, I was really hoping to put that trophy in my shop window. Queen of East Texas Bakers. It would have boosted business a bit, I think."

"Absolutely," he said. "You would have got a nice write-up in the paper, and now you're being cheated out of it."

"Cheated? How do you figure that? You think Ginger's worried that she might not win first prize this year, so she's using Susanna's murder as an excuse to cancel the bake-off so she won't have to give up her trophy? Is that what you think, Al, really? Honestly, sometimes I don't know what I see in you."

He grinned. "You see a man's man. A brawny, sexy hunk of a man that you just can't resist."

She shook her head. "Maybe Caroline's right. I may need to have my head examined."

"No, Caroline's wrong, because remember: I'm always right, baby, and you know it." He went in for a kiss.

She pushed him away. "Not until you brush your teeth. And Ginger hasn't canceled the bake-off yet. Maybe she's gonna take a vote on it."

"Great, because if it's left up to the contestants, I'm sure it won't get canceled."

"Why? Because everybody hated Susanna and they couldn't care less about showing her any respect?"

"No, of course not. They wouldn't say that."

"I should hope not," she said.

"They'll be thinking it, but they won't say it."

She frowned at him.

He said, "Look, all of these contestants have taken half a week away from their bakeries to be here for this thing, and they've probably worked all year to come up with a recipe that might have a chance of beating Ginger's."

"I know I have."

"That's what I'm saying. There's a lot at stake here."

"I know, but . . ."

Al rolled over.

"Wait, don't go back to sleep. You've got to get out of here."

"You're kicking me out?"

"You need to go back to your room and get cleaned up and dressed."

"You're just worried that Caroline's gonna catch us together."

"Just go."

Al lumbered out of bed, pulled on his pants and shirt, and stepped into his shoes. He walked around to Maybelle, leaned down, and kissed her on the cheek. "I had a wonderful night."

"Me too."

He walked to the door.

Maybelle sat up on the side of the bed with her back to him. "See you at the meeting. Eight-forty-five. Don't be late."

"You're not gonna join me for breakfast?"

Without turning her head to look at him, she said, "I don't have much appetite this morning."

"You sure? This restaurant makes a mean sausage omelet and a fantastic Belgian waffle."

"Enjoy." Maybelle stood up and heard Al open the door and say, "Oops, sorry."

"What's the matter, Al?" She turned around.

A woman in the hallway said, "What are you doing here?"

Maybelle winced. It was Caroline. She rushed to the door.

Caroline's fit, five-foot-six body looked like a twig standing next to Al. She squeezed past him and gaped at the bed, which had clearly seen a night of action.

"You're up awfully early this morning, honey," Maybelle said.

"Well, you know what they say: the early bird catches the worm." Caroline sneered at Al.

Al smiled sarcastically at Caroline. "Maybelle, I'll see you at the meeting."

"Okay," Maybelle said.

Caroline closed the door. "Mother, how could you?"

"Now, I don't want to hear any of that."

"Well, you're going to hear it. That man is nothing but trouble. And, besides, you're way out of his league. Can't you see that? He's such a loser."

"How dare you! Al is not a loser. And there are no leagues —not in my world. And I will date whoever I want."

"Date? Are you saying that this is not the first time you've—"

Maybelle smiled proudly.

Caroline turned up her nose and shivered. "That's gross."

"It's none of your business." Maybelle walked toward the bathroom. Then she stopped and looked back at her daughter. "But just for the sake of argument, suppose I told you we've been sneaking around behind your back for months?"

"Oh, Mother. I've warned you about him."

"You don't even know him."

"I know that what he really wants is your money."

"Oh, Caroline. You don't know the first thing about being in love, do you?"

"Don't be ridiculous. I'm forty-one years old."

"So, when are you gonna get a husband? You don't even have a boyfriend."

"I don't need a husband or a boyfriend. They're not worth the trouble. Can you honestly tell me that you wouldn't have been better off without Father?"

"I wouldn't have had you."

"Okay, so you needed him for five minutes. After that, you should have just sent him on his way."

"*Caroline.*"

"And that's exactly what you need to do with Al."

"Shush. Either drop it or go back home and run the bakery. Who did you leave in charge?"

"Frances."

"Good. She'll do fine."

"I hope so," Caroline said. "I probably shouldn't have come."

"Why were you at the bakery 'til midnight last night?"

Caroline sighed. "Because a woman called around eight-thirty and said she was planning a wedding for her daughter and that she wasn't happy with the bakery she'd chosen, and that she needed a five-tier cake and a groom's cake and—"

"When's the wedding?"

"Tomorrow night."

"Are we gonna have to skip out of here and go home to take care of it?"

"Probably not. The woman was supposed to call me back to confirm the order, but she never did. I should have known better. She seemed kind of flighty, but I stayed there for hours waiting for her call anyway."

"Why didn't you forward the calls to your cell?"

"Because my cell service is spotty between here and Tyler. I didn't want to drop the call in the middle of her order."

"That's my daughter. Just so darn conscientious. What am I gonna do with you?" Maybelle hugged her.

"She might call back today."

"Quit worrying about it. You left Frances in charge. If she

doesn't think she can handle the job, she'll turn it down. No big deal. This will be a nice break for you. You spend too much time at work. The only time you ever get away is for your piano lessons. Let's enjoy these few days together. I'm sorry we got off on the wrong foot."

"Well, if it's just going to be the two of us, then I can cancel my room for the next two nights, and we can share your room."

Maybelle smirked. "To keep me and Al apart?"

"Not primarily," Caroline said. "We've been arguing a lot lately and I hate it. I don't want to fight with you."

"Good. Me either. So, you can move in here on one condition: that we don't discuss Al."

"Sold." Caroline glanced at the bed. "But we're gonna need clean sheets and blankets. And fresh pillows."

"Fine."

"And can we please open the windows and air out this room? All I can smell is Old Spice and stale cigars."

"Okay, but not until I get dressed. It's chilly outside."

"Al mentioned a meeting. What was he talking about?"

"Oh, that's right. You're not on Ginger's contact list. She's gonna meet with all of the contestants at eight-forty-five to decide whether to cancel the bake-off."

"Cancel it? I thought we were gonna spend the next couple of days together here. Why is Ginger talking about canceling the bake-off? What happened?"

"I really don't think Ginger will cancel, but there was a murder last night. Susanna Clampford is dead."

"From Susanna's Cakery in Marshall? That Susanna?"

"Yes."

"Oh, my God."

CHAPTER TEN

Thursday, 6:48 a.m.

Ginger didn't slept well, but she woke up early anyway. On weekdays, she and Elijah usually met at seven for breakfast at her bakery. She was afraid he might not show this morning, though, after what he'd learned last night at the hospital.

Jane drove her to Coreyville Coffee Cakes. The line out the front door was much longer than usual.

"Wow," Jane said, "business is crazy—even for bake-off week."

"Probably because they've heard that I'm now a murder suspect."

"So, they're only here to catch a glimpse of the killer? Right."

"Better drop me off in back."

"Okay." Jane took the driveway between the bakery and the wig shop and pulled into the alley. "Now, you call me if you're having any problems, and I'll come right down here and pick you up and take you to the hospital."

"I'm feeling fine. Thanks for the ride." Ginger opened the car door.

"And you're staying with us again tonight."

"I'll think about it . . . Mother."

"I'm serious. You could have a relapse in the middle of the night, and if you're all alone in your house, who would help you?"

"I'm sorry. You're right, of course. See you later. Thanks, Jane." She got out and Jane pulled away.

Ginger let herself in through the back door. Until a few months ago, she would have been walking into the kitchen, but since the renovations, she was standing a couple of yards behind the sales counter. Four employees were helping to-go customers with their selections from the new, larger display cases. Three servers were waiting tables in the expanded dining area.

A woman standing in line called out to Ginger, but she pretended not to hear her and ducked through the doorway into her newly acquired space. The shoe store next door had relocated to a strip mall eight months ago, and Ginger had quickly signed a lease and turned it into a large kitchen and office. Coreyville Coffee Cakes' online store was about to open for business.

Addie Barneswaller, a tall, muscular black woman, was standing in the kitchen giving instructions to two young women in aprons. Ginger and Addie had been close friends since they had taught school together years ago. Then Ginger opened the bakery, and Addie went to work for her. Now Addie was the manager and part-owner of the bakery.

Addie saw Ginger and hurried toward her. "Oh, Ginger, we just found out what happened last night." Addie placed her large hands on Ginger's shoulders. "Are you okay, honey? Why didn't you call me?" She gave Ginger a bear hug.

"I'd already woken up enough people, and besides, my injuries weren't serious—except for some minor memory issues and the fact that I can't smell or taste anything."

Addie released her and stepped back. "Oh, baby doll, no, no, no."

"It's only temporary. I hope. But I hadn't finished creating my recipe for the contest."

"Oh, Ginger."

"I know. I should have had it done a long time ago, but I just have to wait until the inspiration hits me."

Addie grabbed Ginger's arms. "Susanna Clampford. I can't believe she's dead. Now, who'd want to do that? I mean, sure, I know plenty of folks who'd like to have slapped her in the face a few times, but murder?" She shook her head. "What's this world coming to?" She released Ginger's arms.

"I don't know."

"And from what I hear, you like to have got your own self killed trying to help her."

"And the chief thinks I killed Susanna."

"What? That man ain't got half a brain. How'd he come up with that?"

"He thinks we got into an argument out there and that I accidentally killed her."

"You want me to go over there and straighten him out?"

"No. Please promise me you won't say anything to him."

"Well, somebody needs to put his head back on straight."

"It's okay. I'm gonna figure out who the murderer is."

"Ginger goes a-sleuthing? I love it. You're gonna show up the chief again. Just like the other times."

"Well, I might not be as lucky this time."

"You don't need luck, honey. You're good."

"So, how's the training going?"

Addie glanced at the two newbies. "Oh, they're doing just fine. Picking it right up."

"Great. And we may need to hire a few more people if the online business really takes off."

"I predict sales through the roof."

"Here's hoping." Ginger eyed the new ovens and shook her head. "We've invested a lot of money in the online store, and we don't even know what it's gonna do. It may flop."

"Oh, quit worrying, Ginger. It's gonna do great, and we'll be able to pay off the new equipment in no time."

"And cover our lease every month, which is double what it used to be?"

Addie put her hands on her hips. "Well, it's too late to start having second thoughts now."

"You're right. I guess I'm just not myself after last night."

"Yeah, you've been through a lot. But don't you worry about anything, baby doll. We've got it all under control here."

"Okay, good. Thank you, Addie." She hugged her. "I love you. You know that."

"I love you too."

Ginger released Addie. "Now I'm gonna go eat breakfast and try not to think about all this."

"That's a great idea. See you later."

Ginger went back to the other side, walked into the dining area, and saw Jawanda Brown, a young waitress wiping down a table in the corner, waving her over. She spoke to several well-wishers along the way, telling them she was fine. Nothing to worry about.

"Good morning, Miss Ginger. How are you feeling? Is your head still hurting?"

Ginger sat down. "I'm doing much better this morning, Jawanda. Thanks for holding this table for me."

"Of course." Jawanda patted her on the back. "Well, I'm glad you're okay. Will Pastor Bideman be joining you this morning, as usual?"

"I . . . I'm not sure."

"Good morning, Ginger." Elijah walked up to her table.

She smiled. "Good morning."

"Morning, Jawanda."

"Good morning, Pastor."

He pulled out a chair and sat down across from Ginger. "Have you ordered yet?"

"No. I just got here." Ginger looked at Jawanda. "It doesn't really matter which one I get since I won't be able to taste it, but bring me a Sweet Ginger Cake."

"I'd like a . . . Lemon Crunchy," Elijah said.

"And two coffees. Coming right up." Jawanda walked away.

Elijah reached out and took Ginger's hand. "How are you doing?"

She smiled. "Much better now."

"Is your head still throbbing?"

"No. It's not really bothering me much, but of course, I'm on drugs."

"Well, I'm glad they're working."

"I wasn't sure you'd come this morning."

"Why not?"

"You seemed pretty upset with me last night—when you heard about what I'd done, you know, with Lester."

"Because I'd been under the illusion all this time that you were perfect?"

"No, but . . ."

"Okay. I'll admit, it threw me," he said. "Not so much because of what you'd done, but the fact that you'd never told me about it."

"Well, I was embarrassed. And can you honestly say that you've told me everything about yourself?"

"Yes."

"Really? Every little thing?"

"Okay, maybe not every little thing," he said.

"Okay, then."

"Does it bother you?"

"No," she said. "Not really."

Jawanda delivered their mini-loaf coffee cakes and coffees.

"Thanks," Ginger said.

The chief walked up. "I hate to interrupt your breakfast."

"But you're going to," Ginger said.

"I'm afraid I must." He sat down with them.

"Morning, Chief," Elijah said.

"Morning, Pastor. Ginger, are you planning to cancel the bake-off?"

"You're not even going to ask me how I'm feeling?"

"How are you feeling, Ginger?"

"I'm okay. Thanks for asking," she said. "So, you still want me to cancel the bake-off?"

"No," the chief said. "Actually, I don't think you should."

"That's not what you told me last night," she said.

"Yes, I know, but I got to thinking that a lot of folks would be awfully disappointed if you canceled. Some of them look forward to your contest all year long."

She leaned in. "No, that's not it. You just want me to keep my contestants in town so it's easier for you to interrogate them."

He flashed a wry smile. "Oh, I never thought of that."

"What makes you think that one of them is the killer?" Ginger asked.

"Nothing, at this point," the chief said. "But I'd rather it be one of them than be you."

"Well, I appreciate the thought, but I really doubt it's any of my contestants. I sent a text this morning calling a meeting for eight-forty-five so they can vote on whether to cancel or not."

"Well, if you encourage them to go forward with the contest, I'm sure they will," the chief said.

"Probably, but I'm not going to try to push them into it. I need to be sensitive. A woman was murdered. One of our peers."

"I understand, but you really should do whatever you can to keep them in town for a couple more days, for your own sake, because I've got some evidence that points to you." He stood up. "Right now, you're my prime suspect." He turned and walked out of the bakery.

She looked at Elijah. "Well, that's just great."

"Do you think he really believes you did it?" Elijah said.

"I don't know. Maybe he's just trying to get back at me for making him look incompetent during his last two murder investigations."

She began to eat her cake with her fork.

"But in all fairness, both of those cases were pretty tricky." Elijah took a bite of his cake.

"Yet I solved them when the chief of police couldn't."

"Well, what can I say?" Elijah smiled. "You are not incompetent. Besides, this time you're the suspect, and you know you didn't do it."

"As far as I can remember."

He leaned in. "Ginger, no, don't say that. Don't even think it. There's no way you did it."

She took a sip of her coffee, trying her best to taste something. "I've been going over it again and again in my head—what Susanna said when she called me. But maybe I'm not remembering it right. I was wrong about seeing the date of death on my gravestone, so I don't know if I can trust my memories about anything that happened."

"Do you remember taking the shovel out of your shed and carrying it into the cemetery?"

"No," she said.

"That's good. See?"

"I do take it out there occasionally to clean up the weeds around the gravestones—Lester's and mine—but I wouldn't have left it out there."

"When was the last time you did that?"

"A few weeks ago . . . I think."

"And you're absolutely sure you didn't leave it in the cemetery?"

Ginger thought for a moment. "To tell you the truth, I'm not absolutely sure about much of anything right now."

CHAPTER ELEVEN

Thursday, 7:17 a.m.

Bobby Boudreaux's blood pressure was dangerously high.

He could feel it.

He was frantically searching for Al Fenster. He'd already checked the hotel restaurant, and now he was back for a second scan.

He spotted Al sitting in a booth. How had he missed him five minutes ago?

Bobby ran to Al and slid in across from him. He was so out of breath that he could barely speak. "I've been looking everywhere for you."

Al smiled at him nonchalantly. "Well, I've been sitting right here eating breakfast. You hungry? I'll call my waitress." He raised his arm.

Bobby pulled it down. "I don't want anything."

"You sure? The waffles are amazing."

Bobby leaned in. "Tell me."

"What?"

"We were at the bar drinking last night—drinking together, right?"

"Yeah."

"I had too much, man. Why did you let me get sloshed?"

"Hey, it's not up to me to tell a man how much he can drink. I'm not your wife."

Bobby leaned in even closer. "I woke up this morning on my bed and I . . . don't know how I got there. The last thing I remember is that we were sitting at the bar and then . . ." His head began to shake.

"What?"

He whispered loudly and his face turned red. "Nothing! I can't remember anything after that!"

"Well, you sure were angry. You were ranting and raving."

Bobby's eyes widened. "About what?"

"Susanna Clampford."

"Oh, God, don't tell me that."

"Yeah, you were saying how much you hated her because of what she did to you back in your college years."

"College year. It was only one year—thanks to her."

"Yeah, something about her stealing your cake recipe."

"It was the recipe that turned her failing bakery into a success. I got so mad at her that I dropped out of college and never went back."

"Well, that showed her."

Bobby sneered at him. "That woman ruined my life. I was just a kid, and I looked up to her. I wanted to be her—to have my own bakery like her. But she used me. It took me years to get over what she did to me."

"Doesn't seem like you're over it yet."

Bobby scanned the restaurant for cops. He felt a panic attack coming on. "Did you know that Susanna Clampford is dead? That somebody murdered her last night?"

"Yeah, I heard."

"You can't tell anybody, man, the stuff I said about her in the bar last night."

"A lot of it shouldn't have been said in mixed company."

"It was that bad?"

"Yeah, and everybody in the bar heard you."

"I didn't do it, man. You've got to believe me."

"Hey, aren't those the same clothes you were wearing last night?"

"I've got to go." Bobby jumped up.

"Wait. Did you get Ginger's text?"

"What? No. My phone's dead."

"She called a meeting for eight-forty-five this morning in the small conference hall to discuss whether to go ahead with the bake-off or to cancel it—you know, because of Susanna."

"Yeah, okay. Thanks." Bobby turned and hurried out of the restaurant.

CHAPTER TWELVE

Thursday, 7:26 a.m.

Ginger and Elijah finished their breakfast, and he headed for his office at the church. Ginger marched across the street to the courthouse, which sat in the center of town square. She was determined to find out exactly what evidence the chief had against her. Ginger didn't have the patience for the elevator. She took the stairs to the second floor and strode to Chief Foenapper's office.

The chief's secretary said, "Wait. Do you have an appointment, Ginger?"

Ginger swung open his door and walked in. "I want to know what evidence you have against me."

He was sitting behind his desk working at his computer. He didn't bother to look up. "You could at least knock."

Ginger closed the door behind her and walked to the front of his desk, standing over him. "Do you seriously believe that I murdered Susanna Clampford? Seriously? Come on, Chief."

"Settle down, Ginger. Have a seat."

"I don't want to sit down."

"Please."

Ginger sat in a chair in front of his desk. "You can't believe that I did this."

"I'm just following the evidence."

"What evidence? What could you possibly have that makes you think I killed her?"

"You told me that she called you last night around eleven o'clock and wanted to come over to your house to talk."

"When she called, she was already on her way over through the cemetery."

"So, she initiated the meeting. You didn't call her and lure her into the cemetery."

"Lure her into the cemetery? Of course not. Like I told you, she called me."

"Well now, see, Ginger, I can't help you if you're gonna keep lying to me."

She nearly jumped out of her chair. "I'm not lying!"

He shook his head. "We've got Susanna's phone. And there's a voicemail from you that came in at ten-fifty last night."

"Ten-fifty? No. That's impossible. I didn't call her last night. Well, wait, that's not true. She called me and we got disconnected. Then I called her back, but it went straight to voicemail. That's the only time I called her last night—after she called me."

"But how can you be so sure, Ginger, when you're struggling with memory loss?"

Ginger pulled her cell phone out and tossed it on his desk. "Look for yourself, Daniel! Check my call history."

He glared at her.

"Sorry. I didn't mean to throw it at you." She sat down.

He picked up the phone. As he fingered the screen, Ginger wondered if she'd been hasty. What if her mind was playing tricks on her? Maybe she had called Susanna first. But wasn't Fredrick still at her house at ten-fifty, going on and on about his frostings?

"Well, according to your call history, you didn't call Susanna until ten-fifty-six, which was after she called you."

"I told you."

"Wait a second." He glanced at his open notebook. "This is the wrong phone number. Did you call her from your home phone at ten-fifty?"

"No, Chief, I didn't call her at ten-fifty—from any phone. And I rarely ever use my home phone anymore. I've been meaning to cancel the service."

"What's your home number?"

She told him.

"Yep, that's it. That's the number you called Susanna from at ten-fifty—before she called you."

"No, I couldn't have. I'm sure—"

"You didn't call her from your home phone? Or you can't remember calling from it?"

She was confused. Did she need a lawyer? "You said you've got the voicemail I left for her at ten-fifty. Let me hear it."

"Sorry, I can't. The lab's still working with her phone. But I listened to it, and believe me, it's definitely your voice."

"Well, what did I say?"

He picked up his little notebook and read from it. "Susanna, this is Ginger. Would you please come over to my house? I've got something important to talk to you about. I'll meet you halfway on the cemetery shortcut."

"No, no, no. I wouldn't tell her to do that. Not at eleven o'clock at night."

"Well, I'm not making this stuff up, Ginger. That's exactly what you said."

"It doesn't make any sense, though. Why would I leave that message for her, not knowing when she would listen to it, and then head out into the cemetery to meet her?"

"You wouldn't—until she called you back, which you have proof of on your phone, right here in your call history. Susanna called you . . . five minutes after you called her."

"What? That can't be."

"See for yourself." He held up her phone.

"Well, sure. I know when she called me. I remember that. But she called me first, and even when I called her back and it went to voicemail, I just hung up. I didn't leave a message. And just what do you think is my motive for killing her anyway? This thing from college, over forty years ago?"

"I'm still working on your motive."

"Well, let me know when you think you've figured it out."

"Oh, I will."

Ginger stood up and held out her hand. "Could I please have my phone back?"

"Nope. It's got evidence on it."

She shook her head.

"Oh, and something else," he said. "The lab found your fingerprints on the shovel."

"Well, of course. It's my shovel. I'm sure my fingerprints are all over it."

"Yes, but Susanna's blood is on the shovel, and one of your fingerprints is on top of her blood."

CHAPTER THIRTEEN

Thursday, 8:43 a.m.

Ginger left the courthouse and walked over to Coreyville Hotel. She kept thinking about her fingerprint on the shovel—on top of Susanna's blood. There were two possible scenarios: One, she killed Susanna with the shovel, then set it down and maybe checked Susanna's pulse, got blood on her hands, and picked up the shovel. Then, as she was walking away, she tripped, fell, hit her head, and passed out. Or two, somebody had framed her for Susanna's murder.

But if the first scenario was true, then she had serious memory problems, because she didn't remember any of that.

Ginger walked through the hotel lobby, went to the small conference hall, and headed to the front of the room where everyone was gathered near the podium. She saw Marilyn Monastrovi sitting quietly by herself. She had to be hurting. Her longtime boss and mentor had been brutally murdered.

Maybelle Rogers was sitting next to her daughter, Caroline, chatting.

Al Fenster was chewing the fat with Bull Crawley, owner of Bull Crawley's Bar and Grill, which was located next to the hotel. Al was a decent baker. Bull was not.

Cash Crawley, Bull's younger brother and owner of Cash & Carry Donuts, was trying to flirt with Kate Lake, a strikingly beautiful young redhead. Tall, thin, aloof. She looked more like a fashion model than a baker. Cash Crawley's cakes tasted like day-old donuts, but Kate was an up-and-comer and probably posed the greatest threat to Ginger's reign as the queen of East Texas bakers.

Bobby Boudreaux was sitting by himself, nervously jabbing at the screen of his phone, looking as though he'd already had too much coffee. Bobby's Doggers restaurant served delicious food, despite its name, and his bakery had been gaining a reputation for its unique and delectable cakes and pastries.

One contestant was missing, but it was eight-forty-five, time to start. Ginger stepped up to the podium.

Fredrick Marcello scurried in and sat down. Now everyone was present.

"Good morning. First let me say that I know we are all deeply saddened by what happened to Susanna Clampford last night. It's just horrible, and I can't believe something like that could happen here in Coreyville."

"What about you, Ginger?" Maybelle asked. "Are you okay?"

"Thanks for asking, Maybelle. Yes, I'm okay. I was very lucky." She wasn't okay at all, and wouldn't be until she regained all of her memories and her sense of taste and smell, but they didn't need to know about that. "Anyway, my first impulse was to cancel the bake-off."

"No, please don't do that, Miss Ginger," Fredrick said.

She went on. "But I didn't think that would be fair to y'all—for me to make an executive decision. I know you've all worked very hard to prepare your recipes for the contest, and you've set aside these days for the bake-off, so you should be the ones who decide whether we cancel or go forward. Let's discuss it, and then we'll vote. I should tell you, though, that if you do vote to go forward, I will not be participating, except in my role as host. I'm still pretty shaken from what happened to me last night. As I said, I'm okay, but I'll need to take it kind of easy for a few days."

Marilyn Monastrovi stood up. "Ginger, as Susanna's long-time employee and best friend and the manager of her bakery, I'd like to recommend that we go forward with the bake-off. There is no question in my mind that this is what Susanna would have wanted. I will enter her cake for her."

"What about her family?" Ginger asked. "What about . . . the funeral?"

"I'm the closest thing she had to family," Marilyn said. "Everyone else is already gone. I talked to the funeral home this morning and scheduled the service for Monday afternoon, with the viewing on Sunday night. The bake-off will be over by then."

"Okay. Thanks, Marilyn."

Al Fenster stood up. "In light of what Marilyn just said, I agree that we should continue with the bake-off."

Fredrick popped up. "I do too." He sat down.

After a few moments, Ginger said, "Does anyone else have a comment before we take a vote?"

Nobody responded.

"All in favor of going ahead with the bake-off, raise your hand."

Everyone raised a hand.

"Well, okay then." Ginger checked her watch. "You've got about an hour to prepare for your first session at ten. Thanks, everybody."

She stepped away from the podium, and Fredrick pranced up to her.

"Oh, my goodness, Miss Ginger, I'm so sorry about what happened to you last night. I wish I'd stayed at your house a wee bit longer. I could have protected you. Although, I have to admit that I'm just a teensy bit afraid of cemeteries. They give me the willies, you know? But I would have put on my brave face and gone with you. I would have."

"It's okay, Fredrick. Anyway, if you had gone out there with me, you might have been attacked too."

He winced. "Yes, I know."

"Did you notice any other cars on the street when you were leaving my house?"

"No, I don't remember seeing any—not close to your house."

Ginger remembered hearing Fredrick's car drive away right before she got the call from Susanna. Was it possible that he had parked just up the street from her house and then had come back and followed her into the cemetery?

"What kind of car do you drive?" she asked.

"Oh, you've got to see this." He took out his phone, excited like a kid on Christmas morning. "I love Batman, Ginger. Everything Batman, so . . ." He showed her a picture of a fancy sports car with a flat-black finish.

"Wow. Looks expensive. Must have been like a hundred thousand."

"Closer to two. It's a Lamborghini Huracán. It's similar to the model Bruce Wayne drove in the recent Batman movies. And it's the exact same color as his: Nero Nemesis. I love it!"

Obviously, his bakery was doing extremely well—or he was living in his car. "So, you like comic book characters."

"Yes, but Batman's my favorite of all, and he's much more than just a comic book character." He sighed like a teenage girl with a new crush. "When I drive this car, it makes me feel dark and mysterious and dangerous."

Ginger nodded. "Hmm. I'll bet it does."

"I'm thinking about trading it in for the new model, though."

"Fredrick, why did you come to my house last night?"

"You know, to talk about cakes and frosting." He put his phone away.

"And Kate."

He nodded repeatedly in birdlike fashion. "Yes." He seemed to be hiding something.

"And we had a nice talk, but what was the urgency? Why did you have to come at ten o'clock at night?"

"Well, I . . ."

"And what really seems odd about it is that as soon as you left, I got a call from Susanna, telling me she was walking to my house through the cemetery. That's when I went out there and got attacked. Don't you think that's rather coincidental—the timing of it all?"

His eyes jutted from side to side. He looked like he was about to make a run for it. "I, uh, yes, that is . . . interesting.

I'm sorry, Ginger, I've got to go get ready for my session. See you later." He bolted to the exit.

CHAPTER FOURTEEN

Thursday, 9:06 a.m.

Ginger walked out of the room and headed over to Conference Room A, the large one, which had been partitioned into nine areas—one for each contest participant to hold their baking lessons. The hotel provided electrical outlets, chairs, and four eight-foot folding tables that were arranged to form a rectangle. Coreyville Coffee Cakes, sponsor of the bake-off, rented portable ovens, sinks, and refrigerators for each contestant. The bakers brought their ingredients, baking pans, and utensils.

Ginger went to the partition designated for Susanna's Cakery and found Marilyn pulling baking supplies out of plastic boxes to set up for her lesson. Ginger understood why Marilyn didn't want to cancel the bake-off, but she was surprised that she was still going to teach the baking lessons. Maybe staying busy was Marilyn's way of dealing with her grief.

As much as Ginger hated to bother her with a lot of questions, she had to start somewhere, and she figured that Marilyn knew Susanna better than anyone.

"Marilyn?"

She stopped what she was doing and turned around.

Ginger stepped inside the rectangle of tables and walked up close to her. "I'm so sorry about Susanna."

"Thank you, Ginger." She smiled, but there was a touch of sadness in her smile that made Ginger want to hug her. She didn't know Marilyn well, but she imagined that her own daughter, if she'd been fortunate enough to have one, would be lovely like Marilyn.

"Are you sure you're up to this? I mean, everyone would certainly understand if you canceled your lessons."

"No, I don't want to disappoint anyone. Some people drive in from out of town."

"I know. I feel bad about canceling my lessons, but I just couldn't do it. Honestly, I was afraid I might break down in the middle of it."

Marilyn reached out and took Ginger's hands in hers. "Oh, you poor thing. I can't imagine what you've been through. It's a wonder you're even up and walking around." She had soft, caring eyes. It was amazing that working for so many years under Susanna hadn't dampened her sweet spirit.

"I'm actually feeling okay. The only thing that's driving me crazy is that I've lost my sense of smell and taste."

"Oh, no, Ginger."

"But the doctor told me it's only temporary."

"Thank goodness."

Ginger studied Marilyn's face. "I hate to ask, but where were you last night at eleven o'clock?"

"Your hands are all dry and cracked, Ginger. Mine get that way too, working in the kitchen all the time. You feel how soft my hands are? I'll show you my secret."

Was she trying to evade Ginger's question?

Marilyn walked over to her purse, took out a small plastic bottle, and walked back to Ginger. "This is what you need." She opened the top of the bottle, took one of Ginger's hands, and squirted a small amount of liquid into Ginger's palm. Then she used both of her hands to massage it deep into Ginger's skin. It felt amazing, but uncomfortably sensual.

"How does that feel?" Marilyn inched closer and looked deep into her eyes.

"Uh . . . wonderful." The look on Marilyn's face was giving her the creeps. She felt herself wanting to lean back to get a little distance, praying that someone would walk in before Marilyn tried to kiss her on the lips. She could feel herself beginning to blush. Marilyn leaned in even closer, still massaging Ginger's hand. "It's just divine, isn't it?"

Ginger gently pulled her hand away and took a half step back. "I'll bet it's expensive. What is it?" She held her hand to her nose and sniffed it. "What am I doing? I can't smell anything."

Marilyn took Ginger's other hand in hers. "It's olive oil." She poured the oil into Ginger's palm and began to rub it in.

"Just plain olive oil?" Was Marilyn trying to make a pass at Ginger, or was she simply hoping to unnerve her to point that Ginger would forgo any questioning and just get away from Marilyn as quickly as possible? It was surely the latter, which meant she was trying to hide something.

"Extra virgin olive oil from Italy. And I add a few drops of peppermint oil to it."

"It's great. Thank you."

Marilyn finished rubbing Ginger's hand and released it.

Ginger said, "Were you and Susanna staying in a room together?"

"Yes."

"Were you with her last night when she called me? It was around eleven."

Marilyn looked away for a moment. "No. I had gone to the car for a while—Susanna's car. We rode over together. I loved her like a mother, but sometimes she could really get on my nerves."

Ginger smiled. "Like only mothers can."

"Yes. So, I sat in the car for an hour and a half playing a game on my phone."

"Did anybody see you sitting in the car?"

"Oh, you want to know if I have an alibi. Are you investigating Susanna's murder? Am I a suspect?"

"No, I'm just trying to eliminate people from my list."

"You have a list?"

"It's just an expression. I may question every single person in town before I'm done. I want to find Susanna's killer, and I want to know who attacked me."

"I don't blame you. I'd be so angry if someone did that to me."

"So . . . did anybody see you sitting in the car last night?".

"I don't know, but some smokers saw me walk out to the car, and they saw me when I went back into the hotel. Maybe not the same people. I don't know about that. Seems like there are always a few of them hanging around the back door of the lobby, and you've got to pass through their smoke to get to the parking lot."

"I never go out the back door, so I didn't know that, but I'm not surprised since the entire hotel is smoke-free."

"Yeah. So, it was after eleven when I came back to the room, and Susanna was gone. She left me a note saying that you had called her and wanted her to come over to your house."

"What?"

"I gave the note to the police chief."

Ginger looked into her eyes. "Did you tell the chief that Susanna hated me?"

"I don't know if I used the word hate, but yes, I told him that you two didn't like each other."

Ginger shook her head.

"Surely the police chief doesn't think you killed Susanna."

"Unfortunately, he does."

"Oh, Ginger, I'm sorry. That's crazy. I'll go talk to him right now."

"No, you don't need to do that. It wouldn't help anyway."

"I never meant to give him the impression that I thought you killed her. That's terrible. Please let me know if you want me to put in a good word for you."

"Thanks, I will," Ginger said. "Do you have any idea who might have wanted to kill her?"

"Not really, but over the years she made some enemies. She just really knew how to rub people the wrong way."

"How did you stick with her for all this time?"

"As I said, she was like a mother to me, and you don't just give up on your mom. You know, I went to work for her when I was twenty-nine. Now I'm forty-six. I don't even know where all the years went."

"And you never married?"

Marilyn shrugged. "There's never been time for anything but the bakery."

Ginger felt herself pitying Marilyn.

She seemed to sense it and smiled. "Not that I have any real regrets. I love baking and creating recipes more than anything else in the world."

"Oh, I understand that." Ginger smiled and nodded. "What about Susanna's marriage? Were she and her husband happy?"

"They had their ups and downs like every couple. Chuck went through some personal problems a few years ago that caused him to lose his teaching position at ETBU."

"I remember hearing about that. He was a music professor, wasn't he?"

"Yes, and he was a very talented composer. It was so sad when he died."

"That was just a couple of months ago, wasn't it? An accidental overdose?"

Marilyn hesitated. "Yes, that's what they said."

"You don't believe it?"

"Sure. I mean, I have no reason to doubt it, I guess. It's just hard to believe he's gone."

"Did you know him well?"

"I saw him every morning when he'd come by the bakery and have coffee and a sweet roll, and sometimes we'd chat for a while. He was a great guy."

"How was Susanna dealing with his death? Was she depressed?"

"She seemed okay, but maybe she was just doing a good job of hiding the pain. Sometimes I couldn't tell what she was thinking."

"Well, I've taken enough of your time. You've got to bake a cake for your class. I'll let you get back to work."

"No problem. My oven's preheated, and I premixed all of my dry ingredients."

"Well, that's a smart way to do it."

"And listen, Ginger, I'm happy to help you with the police in any way I can. It's ridiculous for them to think that you're capable of murder."

"Thank you, and let me know if you need anything." As Ginger walked away, she looked over her shoulder and said, "Good luck with the contest."

"Thanks."

Ginger wanted to know everything that had been going on in Susanna's life lately, and she felt like Marilyn was holding something back. Maybe the two of them weren't as close as Marilyn said.

Ginger felt naked without her phone, and the chief would probably keep it for days—maybe weeks—but he couldn't stop her from buying a new one. She left the hotel and walked a few blocks to the Verizon store.

CHAPTER FIFTEEN

Thursday, 9:35 a.m.

Ginger left the Verizon store with her new phone, crossed the street, and strolled down the sidewalk to her house. Physically, she was feeling good. Her memories of last night were still swirling around in her head like a nightmare, and her sense of smell seemed close to non-existent, but she was about to put it to the test.

She went straight to her kitchen. It was a mess—just as she'd left it the night before. Bags of flour and sugar, bottles of spices, baking pans, and oven mittens covered her large island. She had been working on dozens of variations of her cake recipe for the contest when Fredrick showed up at her door. Then, right after he left, Susanna had called her, and she had run out her back door into the forty-something-degree night with no coat and a weak flashlight. That part of her memory seemed clear.

Ginger picked up the bag of sugar and opened it. Most

folks couldn't smell granulated sugar unless they snorted it up their nose, but she could pick up the scent from a yard away—normally. She tried it from two feet. One foot. One inch. Nothing. She almost started crying.

But wait! Vanilla. Surely she could smell that. Anybody could smell vanilla extract. She opened the bottle, held it at arm's length, and sniffed. She tried it at one foot. Nothing. She put it right under her nose and inhaled slowly and deeply. She sensed something, or maybe it was just her imagination.

Why was the house so warm? The ovens. Both of them had been on all night. She walked over and turned them off.

Had she even locked the door when she'd rushed out last night? Of course not. This was Coreyville. Nothing to worry about—until now. There was a killer on the loose. Her memories were telling her that Susanna was the one who struck her, but perhaps her mind had inserted Susanna into that memory because it lost the identity of the actual attacker. Susanna hated her, so maybe her brain made the logical substitution.

Ginger locked the back door, walked into the living room, and sat down in her gliding rocker. She considered sitting there until she was completely back to normal—no matter how long it took.

No. That was a ridiculous thought. She was not going to allow herself to fall into depression. No more self-pitying. She took out her new phone and looked up the number for Susanna's Cakery and called it, not really expecting anyone to answer.

"Susanna's Cakery. How may I help you?"

"Oh. I didn't really think y'all would be open today. You know, because of . . . what happened to Susanna."

"Yes, we're all so sad, but we're open so that people can

make donations in Susanna's name for her charity: Cakes for Kids. It was her brainchild—a way to provide designer birthday cakes for the children of low-income families."

It sounded like the woman was reading from written text.

"I see. Well, that's wonderful. Are you also open for regular customers?"

"Yes, we are."

"Okay. Thank you. Goodbye."

Ginger wondered who had made the decision for Susanna's bakery to be open for business on the day after she was murdered. Marilyn? It seemed very odd.

The doctor had not told Ginger it was unsafe for her to get behind the wheel, so she took that as permission to make a drive to Marshall.

CHAPTER SIXTEEN

Thursday, 10:20 a.m.

*G*inger had no problems at all driving to Marshall, but she knew she was going to get a mild tongue-lashing from Jane whenever she found out. And probably from Elijah.

Susanna's Cakery had a lovely facade, and nearly ever parking space was occupied. She pulled in and parked. A sign indicated that there was additional parking in the rear.

When she walked inside, she was blown away by the polished porcelain flooring. It had a mirror-like shine. The dining area was bigger than Ginger's new, enlarged one, and the display cases were longer and taller than Ginger's. Two dozen customers being served by five employees were making selections. There were beautiful cakes, muffins, pies, and various other pastries. Ginger wished she could enjoy the magnificent aroma that surely filled the room.

Ginger looked for an employee that she could approach—

ideally someone who'd been working there for a long time, but they all appeared to be no older than mid-twenties.

A woman said, "You're Ginger Lightley."

Ginger turned to the side and saw a large woman, around sixty, grinning from ear to ear as she walked up to her.

"Yes, I am," Ginger said.

"I'm Dot Harbington, assistant manager. So glad to finally meet you." She was wearing the same type of uniform that the younger women wore—white with gold trim and a tasteful, multicolored Susanna's Cakery logo patch.

"Thanks. And let me offer my condolences for the loss of Susanna. I was surprised that y'all were open today."

"Thank you. It's not easy putting on a happy face today, but Marilyn thought it would be best."

So, Marilyn was still in charge, even though she was out of town. "I understand that you're raising money for Susanna's charity to honor her."

"Yes, and that's a good thing, of course, but it doesn't make it any easier."

Ginger hesitated. "Is there somewhere private that we can talk?"

"Sure." Dot led Ginger into Susanna's office and closed the door.

They sat down across from each other.

"What's going to happen to this place now that Susanna's gone?" Ginger asked.

"Oh, we'll be fine, I'm sure. Marilyn will see to that."

Ginger couldn't imagine that Marilyn had the resources to buy the bakery. She noticed numerous plaques and certificates on Susanna's walls recognizing her community leadership, her sponsorship of a girl's softball team for two decades, her service on the advisory board of the hospital, and many others.

"Looks like Susanna did a lot to support the community," Ginger said.

"Yeah, she was passionate about it. Susanna could be so giving and loving. And she could be hilarious when she wanted to be, especially with her dirty jokes. The women loved her when she was like that. But then she'd turn on you—and be the most hateful and hurtful person you ever knew. I mean, it sounds terrible, but it's just the way she was. I loved her, though."

Obviously, Dot was a gossiper. She wouldn't be timid about dishing the dirt, which was good for Ginger. "I'm afraid the hateful side is mostly what I saw."

"Well, even our sweet Marilyn—saint that she is—got fed up with the abuse sometimes," Dot said.

"But she never quit."

Dot's face lit up. "That's what most people think, but I know better. See, I've only been here for four years, but Susanna and I became very close. We'd sit in this office for hours after closing, drinking and telling stories."

"Just you and Susanna? What about Marilyn?"

"Marilyn's not a drinker, and she didn't approve of Susanna's drinking either. So, Susanna did most of her drinking with me, and she confided in me about everything. And I mean everything."

"So, when did Marilyn quit?"

"About six years ago. She'd been working for Susanna for like ten or twelve years. Susanna yelled at her in a staff meeting, and afterwards Marilyn went to her privately and turned in her two-weeks' notice. Susanna thought she was kidding at first, but Marilyn told her she had a great job offer from a bakery in Tyler."

"Maybelle's Bakery?"

"Yeah," Dot said. "And anyway, she said she was gonna take the job."

"But Susanna talked her out of it."

"It wasn't easy. Marilyn knew she had the upper hand, that without her the place would go straight down the toilet."

"Why?"

"Because Marilyn's the one who creates the original recipes. She's the one with the magic touch. Susanna was a sharp businesswoman and all, but she didn't know squat about baking. And every one of Susanna's employees would quit if Marilyn left."

"Oh, wow."

"Before Marilyn came, this place was struggling. For whatever reason, Susanna had always dreamed of opening her own bakery, but she was just no good in the kitchen. She had one special cake that was real popular, but that was it."

"How did Susanna talk Marilyn into staying?"

"She told her that she was like a daughter to her. But Marilyn told her that words are cheap, so Susanna didn't know what to do. She finally offered to put Marilyn in her will."

"Wow."

"Well, you know, Susanna didn't have any kids of her own, so . . . but she told Marilyn she'd have to agree to never quit—no matter what, and Susanna would have to get her husband to agree to go along with changing the will."

"Chuck."

"Yeah. And he said he would—if Susanna would give him something he wanted."

"What was that?"

"To also add Susanna's niece to their will."

Ginger remembered that in her meeting with the contestants that morning, Marilyn had said that none of Susanna's family was still living. "I didn't know Susanna had any family left."

"Most people don't know about it. Susanna had a half-sister who worked here in the early days of the business, but they never told anybody they were related. That's the way Susanna wanted it. So, her sister got pregnant and the guy skipped town. She had a troubled pregnancy, and around the seventh month, her doctor prescribed strict bedrest. But there was nobody to provide for her. The only thing Susanna was offering was a paycheck—if and only if her sister kept working."

"It sounds like Susanna was hoping she'd lose the baby."

"She was, but the baby survived. The mother died."

"Oh, no. How sad."

"Yeah, and the baby's only family was Susanna, but she refused to take her in, so the kid went into foster care, and she got bounced from one family to another."

"What's her name?"

"Kate Lake."

"Oh, my gosh. Don't tell me that's the Kate Lake who owns a bakery in Longview."

"That's her."

"This is crazy. I can't believe I've never heard about this," Ginger said. "But what happened with the will? You said that Chuck wanted to add Kate to their will."

"Yeah. At the time he and Susanna got married, Kate was a teenager, but when he found out about her, he tried to talk Susanna into adopting her. Susanna said she was too old to adopt, but really, she just didn't want to have anything to do with her."

"So Chuck said that they needed to do something for Kate."

"But Susanna was against it."

"Then how did she hold on to Marilyn?"

"She finally gave in," Dot said.

"So they added Marilyn and Kate to their will."

"Yeah. But, after Chuck died of an overdose a couple of months ago, Susanna told her attorney she wanted to remove Kate from the will."

Ginger shook her head. "What a story. I wonder if she knew she'd been added to their will?"

"Susanna didn't tell her, and Chuck promised that he wouldn't tell her either."

"Any chance that Chuck was murdered?"

"A lot of people around here wondered about that," Dot said, "because of the inheritance."

"What inheritance?"

"Chuck's aunt died last summer and left him nine million dollars."

"Whoa," Ginger said.

"Yeah, and before that happened, Susanna had Chuck on an allowance. He was terrible with money. So when he got his inheritance, he opened a separate bank account and wouldn't let her touch it. She was not happy about that even though she wasn't hurting for money."

"I'm sure the police did a very thorough investigation of Chuck's death," Ginger said.

"Oh, yeah. They were highly suspicious, but in the end, they ruled it an accident. And when Susanna finally got a look at his bank account, she found out that he had made two withdrawals of ten thousand dollars in cash. I mean, why would you need that much cash?"

"Maybe he was gambling," Ginger said.

"That's what Susanna figured because he'd had a gambling problem while he was teaching at ETBU. If he had lived, he might have blown the whole nine million on gambling."

"Where did he die?"

"At his music studio," Dot said. "He gave his lessons at night. Had mostly adult students, I think. Sometimes he wouldn't get home until midnight."

"Wow, that's some awfully late lessons."

"Yeah. Susanna suspected that he was fooling around, but she loved him in spite of it. And then one night, she woke up around two-thirty and realized that Chuck hadn't come home. She couldn't reach him by phone, so she drove to the office building where his studio was. The main door and his office door were both unlocked. His head was on his desk, and she thought he'd fallen asleep or passed out. There was a bottle of rum, a Coke can, a glass, and his pill bottle on the desk. It was empty."

"He was already dead?"

"Yeah. Chuck was addicted to those pain pills. He hurt his back a few years ago when he and some friends were trying to pick up an old piano. He was afraid of surgery, so he got his doctor to prescribe pain meds. One of those opioids. They're so addictive and dangerous—especially when you take them with booze."

"Was Chuck a heavy drinker?"

"Sometimes, socially. But I don't think he ever drank alone—which is why I was surprised when Susanna told me about the bottle of rum in his office, because he wasn't holding parties there. He was teaching music lessons."

"Had he been abusing the pills?"

"Not that I know of. Susanna said he mostly took them when his back pain flared up—usually after picking up something heavy or after sex. But I think their sex life was pretty much over—maybe because of the pain, so . . ."

"Do you know if he'd been depressed?"

"Not as far as anybody could tell, but maybe he was. The medical examiner said he'd taken a bunch of those pills with his rum and Coke. That was his favorite drink."

"Who was his last student that night? Did they see him take any pills?"

"The police never could figure out who any of his students were."

"What? Oh, come on. Surely he had an appointment book," Ginger said.

"Yeah, he kept it in his phone, but all the names were in some kind of weird code, and nobody could ever figure it out."

"How odd." So, what was he hiding?

"Yeah. It sounds like a crazy made-up story, but it's true. Well, let me know if you think of any other questions." Dot stood up. "I've got to get back to work."

Ginger stood. "Okay, I will. Thanks, Dot. It was good to meet you. I hope y'all can keep the bakery going."

"I'm sure we'll be fine."

They walked out of Susanna's office, and Ginger went into the dining area, ready to drive back to Coreyville. She'd lucked into Dot, who'd been a treasure trove of information and handed Ginger a suspect on a silver platter: Kate Lake.

"Miss Ginger?"

Ginger recognized the voice and turned around. "Judy Jo Bailey. Come here and let me hug you." Judy Jo had worked at Coreyville Coffee Cakes during her last two years in high school.

They hugged.

Ginger said, "So, you're a freshman at ETBU this year."

"Yes, ma'am."

"Elementary education, right?"

"That's right. Why don't you sit for a while and I'll buy you a cup of coffee?"

"Oh, I'm not gonna let you buy me anything, sweetie, and besides, my taste buds aren't working right now."

"Really? Is that because of what happened to you last night? Are you okay? You look good."

"Thanks. Yes, I feel pretty good, and the doctor says my loss of taste is only temporary."

"Well, you've got to try our coffee." Judy Jo took Ginger by the hand and led her to a small table. "It just might be strong enough to wake up those sleepy little taste buds of yours."

Ginger laughed and sat down. "Okay. One cup."

"Coming up."

When Judy Jo came back with Ginger's coffee, Ginger said, "So how are you liking the college life?"

"I love it. I'm living in the dorm. I don't really need to, obviously, since I could commute from Coreyville, but I wanted to experience the dorm life, which is one of the reasons I'm working here—to help pay for it."

"Well, that's wonderful. I'm so happy for you." She lowered her voice. "But how are things around here—after what happened last night?"

"It's horrible, and it makes it even worse that everybody's acting like it's just another day. And it feels weird with Marilyn being gone. She's always here."

Judy Jo glanced away for a moment. "Dot's giving me the evil eye, so I'm gonna have to move on, but have the police figured out who killed Susanna?"

"That's why I'm here. I'm doing a bit of sleuthing."

"Oh, wow, like you did last year when that man died at Ginger Bread House? That was so cool how you figured it out."

"The chief thinks I killed Susanna."

"Oh, the chief's a moron. Everybody knows that."

"Well, that's a bit strong, but, yes, sometimes he does need a little help to get it right."

Judy Jo sat her tray on the table and squatted beside Ginger and whispered, "I need to tell you some stuff. It might help you solve the case."

"What is it?"

"It's too much. I can't do it here. I've already been at your table for too long. Besides, somebody might hear me." She checked her watch. "I've got a break at eleven, and I was planning to grab a Big Mac for lunch."

"Well, I wouldn't mind a fish sandwich."

"Good." Judy Jo stood up and walked away with the tray.

CHAPTER SEVENTEEN

Thursday, 11:08 a.m.

Ginger was sitting in a booth at McDonalds, keeping an eye out for Judy Jo Bailey, but thinking that their meeting was going to be a waste of time. Judy Jo had been working at Susanna's Cakery for only a few months. What information could she possibly have for Ginger that Dot hadn't already given her?

Her food was getting cold. She unwrapped her Filet-O-Fish sandwich and took a bite. She couldn't taste the bun. There was no fishiness to the filet. No tanginess to the tartar sauce. Ginger set the sandwich down and took a sip of her diet Coke. Fizzy, but tasteless. She was going to start losing weight fast, and she didn't mind taking off a couple of pounds, but not that way.

Judy Jo slid into the booth, facing her.

"Where's your lunch?" Ginger asked.

"I'm not hungry after all."

"Look, I'm truly sorry about what happened to Susanna. I hope you know that."

"Oh, sure, I know. But why would Chief Foenapper think you were the one who killed her?"

"He found out about the feud between Susanna and me. But that's ancient history."

"The thing about you stealing her boyfriend in college?"

Ginger felt a rush of dizziness. Was it due to her head injury or the thought of the whole world rummaging through her dirty laundry? "How did you know about it?"

"I think everybody at the bakery knows."

"That's weird, because I had a long conversation with Dot right before I ran into you, and she never mentioned it."

"Maybe she just didn't want to upset you."

Ginger shook her head. "So, if Susanna was still talking about me stealing her college boyfriend, she obviously never got over it. I thought she'd been happy all these years—especially after she married Chuck."

"He cheated on her."

"Again?"

"Oh, you're talking about that affair he had with a student a few years ago."

"Yeah," Ginger said, "and that's something else that Dot didn't bring up. I remember reading in the newspaper that the students had voted him professor of the year at ETBU. He taught music theory and piano, I believe. Then, soon after that, I heard he quit his job to write music full time."

"Which was a lie. He was fired because of the affair with that girl," Judy Jo said.

"Well, legally, she was a young woman," Ginger said.

"Yeah. My age. And he was in his forties at the time."

"I'm not condoning it. I'm just saying that they couldn't put him in prison for it. But you're telling me he had another affair recently?"

"Yes."

Ginger thought for a moment. "I certainly hope Susanna didn't think he was cheating with me?"

Judy Jo shrugged. "I don't know who she suspected, but I never believed Susanna's story about how she found Chuck dead in his studio that night."

"What do think happened?"

"I think Susanna got tired of his cheating and went to his studio late that night—maybe she was hiding somewhere, waiting for his last student to leave—and she went in all friendly-like and suggested that they have a drink, and then, when he wasn't looking, she crushed a handful of his pills and stirred them into his drink and watched him die. Then she called the police. That's what I think."

"That's quite a theory, but I'm not sure it helps me solve Susanna's murder—unless . . . do you have any idea who Chuck was cheating with?"

"Yes, but it's a wild guess, so please don't tell anybody where you got it."

"I won't. I promise."

Judy Jo leaned in. "Marilyn."

"No, that can't be right. She's been working for Susanna for years. Susanna was like a mother to her."

"I know. And Marilyn runs the bakery. Not Susanna. She creates the recipes. Not Susanna. And from what I've heard, it's always been that way."

"Yeah, Dot told me the same thing. I was shocked. But

why does that make you think that Marilyn was having an affair with Chuck?"

"Well, just add it up: Marilyn's in her mid-forties and she's never been married. She's a beautiful, sexy woman who doesn't date—as far as anyone knows. Susanna was in her mid-sixties, married to a handsome musician ten years younger than her. Chuck taught private music lessons until late at night when the bakery was closed and Marilyn was at home—or wherever."

"I see what you mean," Ginger said. "But it's all speculation—it doesn't prove anything."

"But let's assume they had a thing going on. Maybe they were even in love. Maybe Chuck was about to divorce Susanna so he and Marilyn could get married. Then Chuck dies of an accidental overdose, but Marilyn suspects—knows—that it's a lie, and that Susanna murdered Chuck, her one true love."

"Hmm."

Judy Jo goes on. "So, Marilyn is filled with rage. She's determined to get revenge. So she waits for the perfect opportunity and murders Susanna."

"And frames me for Susanna's murder? It's possible, but I've got to tell you, I had a very nice conversation with Marilyn this morning, and it's hard to believe that she's capable of any of this."

"I know. She's one of the sweetest people I've ever met, but you've got to admit that it's a possibility."

"Yes. A possibility."

"So . . ." Judy Jo took a folded envelope out of her pocket and slid it across the table to Ginger.

"What's this?"

"Marilyn's spare key. She keeps it in her office. I wrote her address inside."

Ginger picked it up and tried to hand it back to Judy Jo. "No, no. I can't do this."

Judy Jo stood up. "My cell number's in there too. When you're done, pull up to the back of the bakery and text me. I'll come out and get it and put it back. She'll never know."

"No, I just can't."

Judy Jo walked away.

CHAPTER EIGHTEEN

Thursday, 11:33 a.m.

Ginger drove into Marilyn's apartment complex and parked. Was she really going to do this? Breaking and entering? Well, not really breaking since she had a key, but entering illegally. What if somebody saw her going into Marilyn's apartment and reported her?

What if Marilyn drove home between her baking lessons and caught Ginger in her apartment? No, there was no time for that. Marilyn's eleven o'clock lesson would go until noon, and it would take her thirty minutes to drive from Coreyville to Marshall. It was only eleven-thirty. Ginger would be long gone before Marilyn could make it here. But still, she was breaking the law. Not yet though. She was just sitting in her car with the engine running.

A young man walked toward her car.

What did he want?

She hadn't done anything wrong.

Was he going to tell her to roll down her window and ask what she was doing? Which apartment did she live in?

He went to the pickup parked next to her car, got in, and drove away.

Ginger could take the key back to Judy Jo and go home with a clear conscience. She hadn't done anything yet—except take possession of the key. A key that was not hers. A key that she might as well have stolen. She'd already tiptoed into a gray area of the law.

She opened her console and took out a pair of black leather gloves and slipped them on, took a deep breath, got out of her car, and walked toward the building. What would Elijah think if he could see her right now? She put the thought out of her mind.

Ginger prayed that nobody would see her. That she could slip in and out of the apartment without anyone noticing. She stopped at Marilyn's door and took out the key.

A woman came around the corner.

She was walking toward her.

She was talking on her cell phone. To the police?

Ginger was frozen in place. She hoped the woman was talking to a friend, preoccupied with her conversation, so that she wouldn't remember what Ginger looked like, or the fact that she was wearing leather gloves in sixty-five-degree weather.

Once the woman was out of sight, Ginger inserted the key and turned it, opened the door, and slipped inside.

It was pitch black.

Ginger felt for the light switch and flipped it on.

She'd done it. She'd broken the law, and now, regardless of whether she found any evidence, Ginger could go to jail. She looked around the kitchen. It was immaculate. What was she hoping to find that would incriminate Marilyn?

Ginger went into the bedroom and checked the closet. Men's clothing, shoes, slippers? No, no, no. She searched the dresser and the chest of drawers. Nothing.

Finally, she checked the two nightstands, carefully putting everything back as she'd found it. Ginger felt awful about invading Marilyn's privacy. She had no right to go through her things like this. What was she doing here?

But she'd already broken the law and betrayed Marilyn's trust, so she might as well finish. It could be good for Marilyn. Ginger might be able to rule her out as a suspect. She checked the bathroom medicine cabinet. Shaving cream? Aftershave? No and no.

She went back into the kitchen/living area to a small desk. There was a birthday card, a shopping list, and a few bills. Above the desk was a white board with Post-it notes across the bottom of it. They appeared to be from bakery employees.

Happy Birthday, Sweets! You're the icing on everybody's day! —Dot

Happy birthday, Marilyn! I love you. Now give me a raise!!! —Candace

Happy Birthday! Your cupcakes taste like a symphony! —Sharon

happy birthday, girl. you're the best. —Jessica

Happy Birthday! Thanks so much for your patience and encouragement. —Judy Jo

She picked up the birthday card. The front read: *To the daughter I never had*. Marilyn's name had been handwritten at the top of the card. Ginger opened it and read the beautiful sentiment. It was signed: *All my love, now and forever, Susanna*.

Ginger felt like a fool. She had broken the law for nothing. Susanna did love Marilyn like a daughter. Marilyn could not have killed Susanna. No way.

She turned off the lights, slipped out of the apartment, and nearly knocked over an elderly woman. "I'm so sorry."

The woman smiled. "What? I'm fine. You must be Marilyn's sister—or no, maybe her aunt?"

"Uh . . ."

"I guess that was your husband that I met a few weeks ago. Marilyn told me it was her uncle."

Was this Ginger's lucky break? She'd found nothing in Marilyn's apartment and then literally stumbled into this woman and been handed a big, fat, juicy clue. "Oh, right, of course. And when was it that you met my husband? Do you remember?"

"I'm not sure. My memory's not what it used to be." Her eyes glazed over for a moment. "Are you Marilyn's sister?"

Ginger's hopes vanished. For a second, she had thought she was really on to something—that this woman had seen Chuck Clampford come out of Marilyn's apartment, or seen them come out together, and Marilyn had covered by saying that Chuck was her uncle.

The woman looked confused. "So, you're her daughter?"

"Well, it's good to meet you. Bye." Ginger hurried to her car and drove out of the parking lot. On the way to Susanna's Cakery, she thought about what she'd accomplished. She'd gathered a lot of new information about Susanna and Marilyn from Dot and Judy Jo, but her trip to Marilyn's apartment had been a bust. And the clock was ticking. As far as she knew, she was the chief's only suspect, and how long was he going to wait before he decided it was time to lock her up?

She pulled into the back parking lot of Susanna's Cakery and texted Judy Jo.

Within a couple of minutes, Judy Jo came out to her car. "Find anything?"

"Nothing useful." Ginger handed her the key.

"Man, I was so sure you'd find something. Well, you gave it a shot."

"I just hope she doesn't ever find out I was in her apartment."

"She won't. Don't worry. Good luck, Ginger."

"Thanks."

Judy Jo went back inside.

Ginger was about to turn onto the side street when she spotted the chief's car pulling into the front of the bakery. She knew how he would react to Ginger running her own investigation.

She turned the opposite way and prayed he hadn't seen her.

When Ginger got back to Coreyville, she went home. She was discouraged and worn out. She didn't know if it was the head injury or sheer frustration that had drained her energy.

She texted Jane, Elijah, and Addie, and told them she was going to take a nap. She was fine, just tired.

Ginger unplugged the house phone, turned off her cell phone, and stretched out on her bed with a blanket.

CHAPTER NINETEEN

Thursday, 6:42 p.m.

Ginger woke up to a loud sound. Somebody was banging on her front door. It was dark in her bedroom. What time was it? How long had she been sleeping? She sat up and tried to shake off the grogginess.

The banging got louder.

She tried to call out, but her voice sounded weak and hoarse. "I'm coming."

The banging stopped.

Ginger stood up slowly. She felt wobbly.

Something crashed into the front of her house, like a dump truck. The entire house shook, and Ginger fell back onto the bed.

She heard people running into her living room—it sounded like a drug raid.

The overhead lights came on, blinding her.

A man said, "Cuff her." It sounded like the chief.

"Daniel, what gives you the right to break into my house?"

"That's what happens when the police have a warrant and you won't answer the door."

"Well, I was trying to get to the door, but—"

"You're going to jail, Ginger, and then prison, where you belong."

A deputy approached her with handcuffs.

"Stop! I didn't kill Susanna."

He forced her arms behind her back and cuffed her wrists.

Suddenly she remembered everything. Her memories had fully returned, and she could see it all clearly now, like watching a movie: Susanna hit her in the head with the shovel. Ginger was dazed and fell to the ground, face first. But she quickly recovered, rolled to Susanna's legs, and knocked her off balance. Then Ginger got up and wrestled the shovel away from Susanna, who was taller and stronger than Ginger, but Ginger's adrenaline had kicked in.

How dare Susanna try to murder her.

Susanna ran from her, and probably would have gotten away, but she tripped and fell down. Ginger swung the shovel with all her might, bringing it down on Susanna's head with deadly force. Susanna tried to get up, but Ginger hit her repeatedly, until she stopped moving.

She dropped the shovel and knelt down to take a closer look at Susanna. She was not breathing and her head was bleeding. Oh, my God, what had she done? She needed to call 9-1-1, but she didn't. She picked up the shovel and walked up the trail, toward her house. How was she going to get out of this mess? She tripped on the shovel, fell forward, hit her head on something hard, and passed out.

Now she knew the truth.

She had done it.

She was guilty.

She had killed—no, murdered—Susanna.

A debilitating remorse overcame her. She rose slowly to her feet, shoulders drooping, and obediently walked out of the house alongside the deputy, a shell of her former self.

Her head was throbbing, her brain bouncing around in her skull like a basketball rattling in the rim before dropping through the net. What did it matter? She was done. Stab her with a knife, shoot her with a pistol pointblank in the head, take her out with a sniper rifle. It just didn't matter. Her life was over.

Ginger heard banging again. Whatever. She would learn to ignore it and everything else that came her way from now on until she died, a shriveled-up prune of a woman in the corner of her prison cell.

"Ginger!" The shouting voice sounded vaguely familiar.

"Ginger, are you okay?" It was Elijah. Yes, Elijah. Why was he shouting? She couldn't see him. She couldn't see anything.

"Ginger, wake up!"

Wake up? What was he talking about? She was already awake.

Wasn't she?

Her eyes opened, but she saw nothing.

No, wait. There was light at the window. A flashlight.

"Ginger?"

She got up, went to the window, and opened it. "Elijah, oh, Elijah."

"Are you okay, baby?"

She pushed the window screen out of the way and launched herself out the window into his arms. She hugged him tighter than she'd ever hugged him before. "Oh, sweetie, I'm so glad you're here."

"What's going on? What happened to you?"

"The chief and the deputies. They broke down the door and arrested me for murder."

"No, that must have been a nightmare. Your front door is fine. Nobody broke into your house."

"Oh, thank God. But it doesn't matter because my memories came back. I did it, Elijah, I murdered Susanna."

"What? No, you didn't. That was just something else from your dream."

"You think? You really think so?"

"Of course."

"But the way I remembered it in the dream fits with how Susanna was killed and where I was lying on the ground when I woke up afterwards."

"That's because you know how she was killed and where you were when you woke up. Your mind fabricated the dream based on what you already knew. That's why it seemed so real."

"Yeah, okay. That makes sense. You're probably right. Thanks for waking me up."

"Well, it wasn't easy. I was knocking on the front door and then banging, and when that didn't work, I came around to your window."

"I guess my mind turned it into the nightmare. When you were banging on my door, I dreamed it as the police breaking down the door. That's so crazy. I've had nightmares before, but I've never had one that real."

"You've been through a lot in the past twenty-four hours,

what with the concussion and the chief suspecting you of murder."

"Yeah, I guess it just got to me."

"But, Ginger, you cannot tell anybody that your memories are coming back and you think you might have killed Susanna."

"Right. Those memories were only real in the nightmare."

"So, what about right now? Do you remember anything new about last night?"

She thought for a moment. "No, I don't think so, but it's gonna be hard to get that nightmare out of my head. What time is it?"

He checked his watch. "About ten minutes to seven."

"I can't believe I slept so long."

"I've been trying to call you. So has Jane. And Addie was wondering where you were too."

"I turned my cell phone off and unplugged the house phone."

"Well, we were all getting worried."

"I need to get over to the carnival, Elijah, but first I've got to freshen up. Uh-oh. I don't have a key to get back in the house. Would you mind . . . ?"

"No problem." He picked her up and helped her back into the house through the window.

"Come around to the front door and I'll let you in."

CHAPTER TWENTY

Thursday, 7:35 p.m.

*E*lijah drove Ginger to the carnival. On the way over, he got a phone call from a church member whose husband was about to have emergency heart surgery. When he got off the phone, he said, "I'm sorry, Ginger. Wish I could stay with you, but—"

"It's okay, sweetie. I understand. You're needed at the hospital. Thanks for rescuing me from my nightmare. I love you."

"I love you too." He gave her a quick peck on the lips, and she got out of his car.

Elijah drove away, and Ginger walked onto the carnival grounds, paid the five-dollar entry fee, and passed through the gate.

On her way to the area where the bakery tents were, the blaring carnival music and swirling, bright-colored lights made Ginger feel dizzy. She looked down as she walked and took deep breaths.

That morning, Marilyn Monastrovi had seemed like a solid suspect, but after breaking the law and invading the woman's privacy looking for clues and finding nothing, Ginger had put her name on the back burner.

Now she was moving on to Kate Lake. Did Kate know that Chuck Clampford had coerced his wife to add Kate to their will? Was she aware of the fact that when Susanna and Chuck died, she would be receiving a large inheritance? Susanna had talked to her lawyer about removing Kate from the will, but she might not have signed any paperwork yet.

Coreyville Coffee Cakes provided each bakery with a tent from which they could sell their cakes and other products. The bakery owners were all staying at Coreyville Hotel, but their workers would be driving in each night for the carnival, and also on Saturday. The bakery tents didn't produce much profit for the bakeries, but they did provide a valuable promotional opportunity.

The Kate's Kakes tent had a double line of customers in front of it. Kate and three workers from her bakery were serving them. Ginger signaled for Kate to meet her behind the tent and walked around to the door flap.

Kate came out. "Everything okay, Ginger? How are you feeling?"

"I'm doing pretty well. Still not back to normal, but that may take a while."

"So, what can I help you with?"

"I'm sorry, but I have to ask everybody. Where were you last night between ten-thirty and eleven-thirty?"

"I was in my room. By myself."

"Okay. One other thing. Is it true that you're related to Susanna Clampford?"

"No."

"Really? Because someone told me today that your mother and Susanna were half-sisters."

Kate laughed. "What? Who told you that?"

"Well, if you don't mind—who are your parents? Are they still living?"

"I grew up in foster homes, Ginger. Nobody wanted me, but I finished high school and then got out and made it on my own."

"Yes, you've done very well for yourself. No doubt about it," Ginger said. "Did you know Susanna well?"

"Hardly at all."

"Okay. Well, I guess that's it. Thanks, Kate."

"No problem." Kate went back into her tent.

Ginger was stunned. Had Dot Harbington lied to her? Why would she do that? Maybe Susanna had made up the whole story. That didn't make sense either. Of course, if Kate was the killer, she wouldn't want to acknowledge that she was in Susanna's will, but it would come out eventually anyway—assuming it was true.

She went to the Coreyville Coffee Cakes tent and entered from the back. Addie was removing a layer of mini-loaf cakes from a plastic box, and Ginger startled her, almost causing her to drop the cakes. "Oh, my goodness, child, you about scared the chicken livers out of me."

Ginger laughed. "Well, I sure wouldn't want to do that."

"My granny used to say that to us kids." Addie set the cakes on a table. "So, where on earth have you been? Everybody's been looking for you."

"I was at home sleeping. I told you I was gonna take a nap."

"Well, yes, you did, but that was around lunchtime. I sure didn't think you'd be taking a seven-hour nap."

"Yeah, I didn't either, and I'd probably still be asleep if Elijah hadn't come to the house and woke me up."

"Jane and Barb both called me asking about you, then Elijah showed up expecting you to be here, and when he found you weren't and that nobody had heard from you in hours, he went flying over to your house. You should have seen the look on his face, honey. I'm telling you, he was scared to death. I've never seen him like that."

Ginger smiled. "I guess he really does love me."

"That's for sure."

"I just couldn't wake up, Addie. And I was having this horrible nightmare." She told Addie all about it, and by the time she'd finished, she was shaking.

"Oh, honey." Addie put her arms around her and hugged her a little too tightly.

"I can't breathe."

"Oh, sorry."

The chief poked his head inside the back of the tent and startled both of them. "Ginger, I need to talk to you."

"Okay." She stepped out of the tent. "What is going on? Have you got some new evidence?"

"I should be asking you that question. I saw you at Susanna's Cakery today—in the back parking lot."

"I was just there to offer my condolences to Susanna's people."

"Hmm. From what I hear, you were doing a lot more than that."

She hoped he was bluffing. "No, just did a little coffee drinking and chitchatting."

"That better be all. I've warned you about interfering in my investigation."

"I know, Chief. I'm staying out of it."

"Good. So, I do have some new evidence, and it's a blockbuster. It's given me several new suspects."

Great, Ginger thought. Maybe that would let her off the hook. "What is this new evidence?"

"You'll find out tonight."

"It's already nighttime, so why don't you tell me now."

"Later. Ten-thirty in my office. I'm bringing all of my suspects together to hear the new evidence, and that means you too."

"To hear it? So, it's an audio recording?"

He smirked. "I didn't say that, but I'll tell you this: it's gonna blow the walls off this case, and before the night's over, I'll bet somebody's gonna be sitting in jail."

"So I'm no longer your prime suspect?"

"Don't put words in my mouth. Just be in my office at ten-thirty. And don't talk to any of your contestants between now and then."

"So the killer is one of my contestants?"

He looked as if he wanted to strangle her. "Do not talk to them."

"Okay, I won't. I promise."

He walked off.

CHAPTER TWENTY-ONE

Thursday, 10:20 p.m.

Ginger kept her word to the chief. She stayed away from her contestants all evening. But she couldn't sit around and do nothing while Susanna's killer was roaming free, so she walked the carnival grounds, casually visiting with friends to see if they knew anything that would help her solve the case. Her efforts didn't produce any results, but at least it passed the time.

At ten o'clock, carnival closing time, she helped Addie and her workers close down their tent for the night and load the unsold bakery products into a van to be hauled back to the bakery. They would be sold the next day as day-old goods.

Ginger caught a ride with Addie to the bakery and walked across the street to the courthouse. The chief's meeting was scheduled to start in ten minutes.

Apparently, his plan was to play some audio recording for the group and magically flush out the killer. She was doubtful that it would work—not because it was impossible to have success with that technique, assuming the contents of the recording were sufficiently incriminating—but Ginger just didn't think the chief could pull it off. She hoped she was wrong, though, because nothing would make her happier than for the killer to get caught—no matter who got the credit.

The chief's receptionist had gone home hours ago and his office door was wide open, so Ginger walked in. The chief was sitting behind his desk with seven chairs lined up in a row facing him.

"So, seven suspects?" Ginger asked.

The chief looked up. "Including you."

"But I thought you said—"

Kate Lake walked in. "Hello, Ginger."

"Hi, Kate."

"Any idea how long this is going to take, Chief?" Kate asked.

He smiled at her and stood up. "We'll get going just as soon as everybody's here, Miss Lake. Please have a seat. Can I get you anything? Bottled water? Coffee?"

The way he was looking at her, Ginger thought he might offer his shirt, his car, and his bank account.

"No, thanks. I'm fine." She sat at the end of the row.

Fredrick Marcello was next in. "Hello, Miss Ginger."

"Hi, Fredrick," she said.

"Have a seat, Mr. Marcello," the chief said.

"Thanks." He went directly for the chair next to Kate's, but she gave him a cold stare, and he retreated to the opposite end of the row.

Ginger heard someone talking and looked back. Maybelle

Rogers and Al Fenster had just walked into the receptionist's room.

"I told you it was down here," Maybelle said.

"Well, according to the sign, it should have been the other way."

"Hello, everybody." Maybelle grinned as they walked into the chief's office.

The chief nodded to them. "Mrs. Rogers, Mr. Fenster, please have a seat."

Ginger greeted them.

Fredrick said, "Hi, y'all."

Kate was playing with her phone.

Marilyn walked in. "I guess this must be the place."

Ginger gave Marilyn a warm smile, hoping to conceal her guilt over snooping around in Marilyn's apartment. "Hi, Marilyn."

"Hello, Ginger."

The chief smiled at her like they were old friends. "Please have a seat, Marilyn." He picked up his little spiral notebook. "So, let's see . . . who are we missing?"

"That would be me." Bobby Boudreaux rushed in carrying a tray covered with foil. "I've got muffins if anybody's hungry."

"Let's get started," the chief said.

Bobby set the tray on the corner of the chief's desk, pulled out a muffin, sat down, and began devouring it.

The chief frowned at Bobby, but he didn't seem to notice.

Ginger took the remaining chair, next to Fredrick.

The chief said, "I called y'all here tonight because I have some new evidence pertaining to the murder of Susanna Clampford, and it involves every one of you."

Kate jumped in. "Well, that makes no sense, Chief, because I had absolutely nothing to do with it."

"Me either," Al said.

"Oh, really?" He read from his notes. "On March seventh, just over two weeks ago, Susanna Clampford held a meeting at her bakery with everyone who's sitting here—except Ginger. Anybody gonna deny that?"

No one responded.

The chief went on. "Good, because I've got you all on this recording—except for Ginger and Marilyn." He held up a handheld digital recorder.

"Where did you get that?" Kate asked.

"What does it matter?" the chief said. "It's your own words that condemn you. I'm going to play this, and I don't want any comments until it's over. Understood?"

Everyone nodded.

"This recording was made after Susanna Clampford left the room." He set the recorder on the edge of his desk and pressed the play button.

Kate: "Hah! That woman's crazy if she thinks I'd ever sell my bakery to her."

Fredrick: "I'm with you, girl, all the way. She needs to have her head examined, and I'll bet there's nothing but a little tart bouncing around in there."

Kate: "She is a little tart."

Al: "A big tart."

Bobby: "A pop tart."

Kate: "What does that even mean, Bobby?"

Bobby: "I don't know. I just thought it sounded funny." He cleared his throat. "Personally, I think her head's filled with meringue."

Maybelle (while laughing): "Oh, she's not that bad. Look, y'all, she's gonna make us an offer. Fine. We don't have to accept it."

Al: "We don't even know how high she'll go. Not very, I'm guessing."

Maybelle: "But, you know, she recently came into some money."

Al: "Yeah, her dead husband's inheritance money."

Kate: "Well, I don't care how much she offers me. I'm not selling her my bakery."

Bobby: "Are you sure? Not even for a million dollars?"

Kate: "Hey, she may be crazy, but she's not gonna overpay us. And don't forget what she said about the non-compete clause. There's no way I'm moving a hundred miles away to open another bakery. I know people in Longview, and they know me and like me. My place is getting a reputation as the best bakery in town."

Fredrick: "Uh, maybe second best."

Kate: "Keep dreaming the dream, Fredrick. What I'm trying to say is that with Susanna—now that she has money—if we don't sell out to her, what's her next move?"

Bobby: "I know what she'll do if I don't sell to her. I know exactly what she'll do. She'll open her own bakery across the street, undercut my prices, and—"

Al: "And start a rumor that the health department found dead rats in your kitchen."

Bobby: "Right. She plays dirty."

Al: "Worse than dirty. Nasty. If she decides to go after you, you're as good as dead. She'll destroy your business. I'll guarantee you that."

Maybelle: "Well, I don't want to sell either. There's got to be something we can do to stop her."

There was a long pause on the recorder, and then Kate's voice was heard again.

Kate: "We could kill her."

Laughter rang out from the group.

Kate: "No, really. Think about this: Ginger Lightley's Annual Bake-Off is coming up in two weeks. Is everybody going?"

Everyone could be heard replying affirmatively.

Bobby: "Hey, we could do it in that cemetery behind Ginger's bakery. You know? Lure Susanna out there late one night and—"

Fredrick: "Hit her over the head with a rock."

Kate: "But we'd need to frame somebody for the murder so the police wouldn't come after us."

Al: "Ginger."

Again, laughter rang out.

Bobby: "That's crazy. Nobody would believe Ginger Lightley would murder anybody."

Maybelle: "I don't know, they might, if they knew the dirty little secret I know."

Fredrick: "What is it? Tell us."

Maybelle: "Well . . ." There was a long pause. Then, "When Susanna and Ginger were in college, Ginger stole Susanna's boyfriend."

Kate: "Oh, big deal."

Maybelle: "By sleeping with him."

Kate: "Oh."

Maybelle: "And then marrying him. But Susanna was still in love with the guy, and she's hated Ginger ever since."

Bobby: "Oh, we can use that, baby. But how are we gonna get Ginger and Susanna in the cemetery at the same time?"

Kate: "I could call Susanna and pretend to be Ginger—you know, spoof the phone number to make it look like Ginger's calling her."

Fredrick: "Do the voice, Kate. It's hilarious, y'all. Show them how you can do it."

Kate: "Okay, okay." There was a long pause, then Kate, sounding eerily like Ginger: *"Hello, Susanna, this is Ginger Lightley. Would you mind coming over to my house? I've got something important to talk to you about. And take the shortcut through the cemetery. It's much faster."*

More laughter could be heard.

Al: "Dang it. You sound just like her. That's crazy. Can you do other voices? Anybody famous?"

Fredrick: "No, do Susanna."

Kate (sounding like Susanna): "I don't think I care for the tone in your voice, Ginger, but I'll meet you out there in the cemetery anyway, because I've got a few bones to pick with you, sister."

More raucous laughter.

Bobby: "That's amazing, Kate. How do you do that?"

Maybelle: "I hate when Susanna calls me sister. I am not her sister, and I thank the Lord above for that."

Bobby: "Nobody would want Susanna for a sister. What a curse that would be. Can you imagine growing up in the same house with that woman?"

The chief pressed stop on the digital recorder.

Ginger stood up and faced the other suspects. "The five of you conspired to murder Susanna and frame me. How could you do that? What did I ever do to deserve this? What did Susanna do? Well, she did a lot, I guess, to make people hate her, but she didn't deserve to die for it. And I didn't deserve to be assaulted and nearly killed. Do you have any idea what

I've been through? I've got memory loss. I can't taste or smell anything."

"I'm sorry, Ginger, but we were just joking around," Fredrick said. "We had nothing to do with what happened to you and Susanna. At least, I didn't."

"Ginger, you don't think we'd really do any of that, do you?" Bobby said.

"I wasn't even in the room," Marilyn said, "so I don't know why I was invited to this meeting. I didn't know anything about this plot."

"It wasn't a plot," Kate said. "It wasn't anything real. We were just blowing off steam."

"Sounds to me like you're all guilty," the chief said. "Except for you, Marilyn."

"And me!" Ginger said.

The five talked at once, denying any involvement in the murder.

The chief held up his hands. "Anybody got something else you want to tell me?"

They were murmuring among themselves, but nobody was talking to the chief.

"Okay," the chief said. "That's all for now—except for this: do not leave town until the bake-off is over."

Ginger was shocked and disappointed that her fellow bakers had so little respect for her that they would laugh about framing her for murder. She believed their claim that it was a joke—at the time. But what if they'd later decided it was a viable solution to their problem?

CHAPTER TWENTY-TWO

Thursday, 11:22 p.m.

*A*fter having such a horrible nightmare that afternoon, Ginger knew she wouldn't want to sleep alone tonight. Besides, she had a lot to discuss with the girls. She called Jane and asked her to pick her up at the courthouse and take her back to Ginger Bread House. Jane wanted to hear all about Ginger's day, but Ginger told her she wanted to wait and share it with Barb and Ethel at the same time, so Jane gave her a quick report on the activities at Ginger Bread House. It was boring stuff, but Ginger didn't mind. She'd already had enough excitement for the day.

By the time they arrived, all of the guests had retired to their rooms for the evening, so the girls went into the office and took their seats around the coffee table.

"Jane told us about the chief rounding up all his suspects," Barb said.

"Yeah," Ginger said, "he thought he was going to solve the

case tonight. He was so confident. And the recording was shocking. It made them all look bad, but it didn't prove anything." She told them about what was on the recording.

"I just can't believe they were joking around about killing her," Barb said, "and framing you for it. Even if they had nothing to do with what happened, they should all be ashamed of themselves."

"Oh, they were—except for Marilyn," Ginger said. "She wasn't in the room when they were saying those things. Susanna and Marilyn had stepped out to let them discuss it among themselves."

"Well, what I want to know is who made the recording?" Ethel asked.

"I guess it was whoever gave it to the chief," Ginger said, "and he wouldn't say who that was."

"Had to have been one of the people in the room tonight," Jane said. "Don't you think?"

"Most likely," Ginger said, "which makes me think it was Marilyn. Maybe Susanna had the room bugged so she could find out what the others really thought about her offer to buy their bakeries. And Marilyn was like a daughter to her, so I'm sure she would have shared it with her."

"How do you know that Marilyn was so close to Susanna?" Barb asked. "I didn't think you knew Marilyn very well."

Ethel said, "Everybody knows that Marilyn's been working for Susanna since she was a teenager."

"Actually, she was twenty-nine," Ginger said.

"Ginger's been doing her homework," Jane said. "She drove over to Marshall this morning and talked to some of the workers at Susanna's Cakery."

"Oh, good," Barb said.

"Good and bad," Ginger said.

"What does that mean?" Ethel asked.

Ginger hesitated.

"What is it, Ginger?" Jane asked.

"I broke into Marilyn's apartment," Ginger said.

Jane's eyes widened. "What?"

"No," Barb said.

"She's kidding," Ethel said. "Right, Ginger?"

"Technically, I didn't break in," Ginger said. "I borrowed a key."

"From Marilyn?" Ethel asked.

"No," Ginger said.

"Oh, Ginger," Jane said.

Ginger pointed to each of them. "The three of you are sworn to secrecy. Agreed?"

They nodded.

"What would possess you to do something like that?" Barb asked.

"I heard a rumor that Marilyn was having an affair with Chuck Clampford," Ginger said.

"Susanna's husband?" Barb asked. "Oh, now we're getting somewhere."

"But I didn't find anything incriminating in her apartment," Ginger said. "I thought I might find something to prove that Marilyn and Susanna weren't really friends, that it was all for show, and that they secretly hated each other. Instead, I found a birthday card from Susanna with a lovely, heartfelt sentiment that kind of . . . got to me. As I was reading it, I felt sad that I'd never had a child of my own."

"Oh, sweetie." Jane reached over and squeezed Ginger's hand.

"So, as for the recording," Ginger said, "it would make sense that Marilyn gave it to the chief to help him nail the person who murdered her best friend, Susanna."

"Yeah, seems like Marilyn's the only one who could have given him the recording," Barb said.

"Unless the chief found it in Susanna's things, or in her office at the bakery, or even at her house. I'm assuming he got a warrant to search her home. I know he went to her bakery because I saw him there, and unfortunately, he saw me, or somebody told him I was there. He was not happy with me tonight."

"Back to the recording," Jane said. "If they were just joking around, I wonder why the chief thought it was important to the case."

"Well, for one thing," Ginger said, "the chief told me this morning that he's got me on Susanna's voicemail asking her to come to my house by way of the cemetery shortcut. But I never left her a voicemail. I'm sure of that."

"You think he suspects that it was Kate Lake who called Susanna, impersonating your voice?" Barb asked.

"Maybe," Ginger said. "She does it well. I could barely tell that it wasn't me. I'm sure Susanna would have been fooled."

"Unless she'd already heard Kate do your voice on the recording," Jane said.

"Right," Ginger said. "So maybe Susanna didn't know about the recording."

"Well, even if you believe they were only joking around," Barb said, "what if a few days later they decided to do it for real?"

"I've considered that possibility," Ginger said. "Let's say that Kate called Susanna, pretending to be me. At that same time, Fredrick was at my house. Then he left and Susanna called me from the cemetery."

"Or was that Kate calling you, pretending to be Susanna?" Jane asked.

"But can't the police see who made the call?" Ethel said. "Doesn't it show right there in the Caller ID?"

"There's a way to fake that," Barb said. "It's called 'spoofing' the Caller ID. Remember when I got that call from the bank asking me for all kinds of information? The Caller ID said it was the bank, but it was really some scam artist trying to get my personal information so he could steal my money."

"Oh, yeah," Ethel said. "I remember that."

"So let's just assume that Susanna called and you went into the cemetery to find her," Jane said.

"But it couldn't have been Fredrick who killed Susanna and attacked you," Ethel said, "because he'd just driven away from your house in his car."

"Yeah, but he could have parked his car a couple of houses down and then followed me into the cemetery, knocked me out, and killed Susanna," Ginger said. "Of course, I keep thinking that it was Susanna who hit me with the shovel, but it was dark and, as I keep saying, my memories are still fuzzy, so I'm not sure."

"But he could be the one," Ethel said.

"Even if he wasn't the one who killed Susanna and attacked Ginger," Jane said, "he could have just been there to make sure Ginger stayed home and didn't come over here for the night, and that she stayed awake for the call. Susanna didn't call until nearly eleven, and Ginger could have already been in bed asleep."

"I really need to investigate all of them," Ginger said. "And would y'all mind making some calls tomorrow to see what you can find out? Even if it's just rumors, it might help."

"Sure," Jane said.

"I'll get on it in the morning," Barb said.

"Me too," Ethel said.

"Will one of you call all the people in my immediate neighborhood and ask if they saw a black sports car parked on the street last night after eleven o'clock?" Ginger asked.

"Sure, I'll do it," Barb said.

"Thanks," Ginger said.

The doorbell rang.

"Who in the world could that be at this hour?" Jane got up. "They're gonna wake the guests."

Barb and Ethel popped up too.

"I don't know," Ginger said, "but it's probably for me." She got up and followed Jane to the front door.

Jane peeked out the sidelight and said, "It's Boot Hornamer." She opened the door.

Ginger stepped up beside Jane. "What's going on, Boot?"

"Mind if I come in?"

Ginger was always leery about allowing Boot indoors when he had a wad of tobacco in his cheek, but she let him in anyway.

"Hello, ladies." He nodded. "Sorry to bother you so late, but I figured Ginger would want to know about this. Chief Foenapper just found out that Susanna's deceased husband was having an affair."

"Chuck Clampford," Ginger said. "Yeah, I heard the rumor. How did the chief find out about it?"

"He said that Marilyn woman told him after the meeting," Boot said.

"Really?" Ginger asked. "Marilyn told him about it? That's surprising."

Boot went on. "So now he's got this crazy theory that you were the other woman."

"What? That's outrageous!" Barb said. "Tell him, Ginger."

Boot said, "And he figures that's why you and Susanna got into a fight in the cemetery and you accidentally killed her."

Ginger was stunned.

"That's ridiculous," Barb said. "Tell him, Ginger."

Ginger finally blurted, "Of course it's ridiculous. I didn't even know Chuck Clampford."

CHAPTER TWENTY-THREE

Friday, 9:27 a.m.

*G*inger woke up refreshed, but only because the girls let her sleep in. She skipped breakfast and asked Jane to drive her to Coreyville Hotel.

On the way over, Ginger said, "I can't believe that the chief suspects me of having an affair with Chuck Clampford. Does he really think I'm capable of that?"

Jane said, "Well, he thinks you're capable of murder, so . . ."

"But he knows I've got Elijah. He's my boyfriend."

"Why do you suppose Marilyn told the chief about Chuck's affair anyway? To throw suspicion away from herself?"

"It's possible," Ginger said, "but I already kind of marked Marilyn off my list of suspects. If there was an affair, the mistress could well be the murderer, but I don't think it was Marilyn."

"It does seem odd, though, that she would give the chief a

recording that made everybody look guilty—whether they were joking or not—and then tell him about the affair. If she believed that somebody on the recording killed Susanna, why muddy the waters?"

"That's a good question, Jane."

Jane pulled up in front of the hotel and Ginger got out.

"Good luck, Ginger."

"Thanks."

Ginger walked into the hotel, trying to decide which of her contestants to talk to first. She wondered why the chief invited Marilyn to the meeting last night. Was it because it was her recording? Maybe it was so she could speak to the context of the meeting in case someone tried to misconstrue the facts. Everyone seemed to believe that Susanna made the recording to find out what the bakers really thought about her interest in buying their bakeries.

But what if someone other than Marilyn or Susanna recorded the conversation and gave it to the chief—someone who was on the recording? Who would do that? She had no idea, so she was going to ask everybody, starting with . . . Maybelle Rogers. It was a random choice, but she had to start somewhere.

Ginger walked up to the desk clerk and asked for Maybelle's room number. She took the elevator, went to Maybelle's room, and was about to knock when the door opened. She was facing a woman's back. Ginger recognized the voice as soon as the woman spoke. It was Caroline Rogers.

"I'll see you downstairs, Mom." She turned around and was startled to see Ginger standing in the doorway.

"Sorry, Caroline. I was about to knock."

"That's okay. You just surprised me. Are you here to see me or Mom?"

"I was hoping to speak to your mother."

Caroline looked back. "Mom, Ginger Lightley's here, and she'd like to talk to you."

"Okay." Maybelle sounded like she was in the bathroom with the door open. "Invite her in."

Caroline stepped back, and Ginger walked into the room. "I'm gonna go downstairs and start setting up for our sessions."

"Okay," Ginger said. "I won't hold up your mom for long."

Caroline left.

Maybelle walked out of the bathroom. "I'm in the middle of doing my makeup, so please excuse my face. We're running a little late this morning because we lazed around and had a room-service breakfast."

Ginger looked around the room for clues. "So, Caroline's rooming with you?"

"Yes."

"Hmm. I looked over the reservations Wednesday morning, and I remember seeing that Caroline had her own room."

"She did, but she canceled it and moved in with me yesterday." She hesitated. "Caroline and I have been arguing a lot lately, so she wanted her own room. But, well, we've kind of made up."

"Oh. Good. I see that you two enjoy a good Pinot Noir." Ginger pointed to the bottle on the table.

"I do. Caroline hates wine. She prefers mixed drinks."

"Well, this won't take long. I just need a little help—"

"With the murder case?"

"Yes. I'm trying to put all the facts together and I—"

"You're really good at this amateur sleuthing thing, aren't you? A regular Jessica Fletcher."

"Oh, I wouldn't go that far," Ginger said. "I've had some luck in the past, but not too much this time—so far."

"Well, how can I help?"

"Where were you Wednesday night between ten-thirty and eleven-thirty?"

"Uh . . . lying in bed watching TV."

"Anybody in the room with you?"

"No. At that time, Caroline was still in Tyler and Al—I mean, I was alone."

"Caroline was still in Tyler at eleven-thirty?"

"Yes. She's kind of a micromanager and a workaholic. She's always been that way. Caroline's got a degree in mechanical engineering, you know."

"No, I didn't know that."

"Yes, from Texas Tech," Maybelle said. "After she graduated, she got a great job with a big company in Dallas. But then I had my breakdown when my husband left me for another woman."

"I'm so sorry."

"That was fifteen years ago, and Caroline's been working at the bakery ever since. Running it, really, from the first day she walked in."

"I see. Well, I have a question about the recording we heard last night in the chief's office. Are you the one who made it and gave it to the chief?"

Maybelle chuckled. "I see how you get results. Your questions are very direct."

"I hope you'll be just as direct with your answers."

"Well . . . yes, I recorded it with my phone. How did you figure it out?"

"Lucky guess."

"Isn't that cheating?"

"Not really. Whatever works."

"I felt that I had to turn it over to the police after what happened to you and Susanna. We shouldn't have been talking like that—even though we were just joking around."

"You think one or two of the people on that recording might have turned the joke into something serious?"

"I don't know."

"But isn't that why you gave the recording to the chief?"

"Well, sure. I mean, what if I'd kept it a secret and, because of me, the killer got away with it? I couldn't live with that hanging over my head."

"What about Caroline? I didn't hear her voice on the recording, but was she there for the meeting?"

"No. In fact, Caroline's never been to Susanna's Cakery, as far as I know. She rarely even goes to Marshall at all—well, except for . . ."

Maybelle looked like she'd just said more than she should have.

"Except for what?" Ginger asked.

"Her piano lessons. But please don't tell anyone. She's embarrassed about it. She thinks she's too old to be taking piano."

"Why? A lot of adults take piano."

"Yes, but she had a terrible experience as a child, and it was really my fault. I set her up for failure, making a big deal out of her recital, inviting all of our friends and family to see our amazing daughter perform. She was really quite good. My husband and I thought she might grow up to be a professional musician."

"But she bombed."

"She went blank. Poor little thing couldn't remember a note. She just sat there staring at her fingers on the keyboard, as though they knew what to do but just wouldn't do it. She jumped up and ran out of the room and cried her eyes out."

"And never took another lesson."

"Not until about a year ago. I don't know what made her decide to give it another try, but she seems to love it. And would you believe she's taking lessons from the same teacher who taught her as a child? Back then, the woman lived in Gladewater where we live, but now she lives in Marshall, so Caroline drives over there every Tuesday and Thursday evening."

"Wow, that's an hour drive one way," Ginger said. "She must be serious about it."

"She is. And I'm thrilled because Caroline desperately needs some outside interests. She loves managing the bakery, but there's got to be more in her life than running a business."

"She's not married? No kids?"

"And no grandkids for me. She says she's given up on men."

"That's too bad. She's so beautiful, and she's still young."

"Forty-one."

"I would have guessed thirty-five, tops."

Maybelle smiled. "I'll tell her you said that."

"But getting back to the recording . . . would you mind if I listen to it again?"

"Well, Ginger, I really need to get downstairs."

"I just need to hear the last couple of minutes."

"Yeah, okay, then." She walked over to the nightstand, picked up her phone and ran her fingers across the screen for a few moments, and then handed the phone to Ginger. "You can take a quick listen while I finish my makeup."

"Great. Thanks."

Maybelle went into the bathroom, left the door open, and began applying more makeup.

Ginger started playing the recording near the end and then quickly brought up various apps, looking for evidence—although she had no idea what she was looking for. She scanned Maybelle's recent email and her texts, but there wasn't much there. Then she checked her browser history. Nothing of interest.

Realizing that the recording was near the end and that Maybelle was nearly finished with her makeup, she began to randomly open apps. She was getting nowhere—until she opened Google Earth. The location that popped up was Old Coreyville Cemetery. She could see the shortcut trail between her house and the alley behind her bakery.

Maybelle said, "Well, that's about the best I can do." She walked out of the bathroom.

Ginger closed the Google Earth app and reopened the audio player just as the recording came to the end. She held out Maybelle's phone. "Thanks so much for letting me listen."

"I hope it was helpful to you."

"I think it will be."

"Well, I need to go."

"Of course." Ginger followed Maybelle to the door. "Just one more thing, if you don't mind."

Maybelle turned. "What's that?"

"What's the name of Caroline's piano teacher?"

Maybelle seemed uncomfortable with the question, and for a moment, Ginger didn't think she was going to answer.

"Sarah Baldwin."

Ginger knew she could easily remember that name. Baldwin was the maker of her grandmother's piano—the one sitting in her living room that she never played.

Baldwin.

Sarah Baldwin.

CHAPTER TWENTY-FOUR

Friday, 9:52 a.m.

*G*inger rode the elevator down to the lobby with Maybelle, and then they parted ways. She wasn't sure that Maybelle had been entirely truthful with her—especially when Ginger asked for the name of Caroline's piano teacher. She'd hesitated. Why? It seemed like an innocuous question. Ginger wasn't even sure why she'd asked. Perhaps there had been something about Maybelle's account of Caroline taking piano lessons that didn't ring true. Regardless, Ginger figured she could easily verify the story with a quick phone call.

What was the teacher's name? The same as the brand of her grandmother's piano: Baldwin. First name? Susie. No, Sarah.

She went out the back door of the lobby into a cloud of smoke, causing her to cough. There were three hotel workers sitting on benches, chatting and blowing billows of smoke into the fresh spring air. She continued to the parking lot and stopped near a lamppost.

Ginger took out her phone, opened the browser, and looked up Sarah Baldwin's number. She checked to make sure no one was within earshot and called the number.

"Hello?" The woman's voice was faint.

"Is this Sarah Baldwin?"

"Uh . . . yes." She sounded like she'd just woken up from a long nap.

"Hello?" It was a different voice. Younger sounding. "This is Sarah's daughter. May I help you?"

"Your mother teaches piano lessons, right?"

"I'm sorry. Not anymore."

"Oh, I see."

"I've been meaning to disconnect her home phone so we don't get these calls." It sounded like she was walking into another room. "She's just not herself anymore. It's Alzheimer's."

"Oh, I'm so sorry. When did she stop teaching?"

"At the end of last summer. She wanted to go on, but . . ."

"Well, I'm sorry to bother you, but do you know if your mother had a student named Caroline Rogers?"

"No, I don't know. Did you need a recommendation?"

"Have you ever recommended Chuck Clampford?"

"Well, yes, but . . . he died."

"Yes, I know. Thank you so much."

Ginger said goodbye and hung up.

She thought about what Maybelle had told her—that Caroline started taking lessons from Sarah Baldwin about a year ago, which would have been March or April, so that was possible. But she'd given the impression that Caroline was still taking the lessons.

Had Caroline switched to a different teacher—Chuck Clampford—without mentioning it to her mother? Or was Caroline lying to her mother about the whole thing? Was she driving to Marshall on a regular basis to do something completely different? Or was she even going to Marshall at all? Was Ginger wasting her time pursuing something that had nothing to do with the murder?

Her phone rang.

"Hello, Chief."

"Ginger, I've got some new evidence I want to show you. Can you come to my office?"

"Right now?"

"Yes, please."

"I'm right across the street at the hotel. Be there in five minutes."

It was uncharacteristic of the chief to go out of his way to share evidence with Ginger. He always wanted to solve the crime before she could figure it out, so why was he offering to help her?

CHAPTER TWENTY-FIVE

Friday, 10:10 a.m.

Ginger walked into the chief's office. "I want to set one thing straight right now. I did not have an affair with Susanna's husband, and I can't believe you would think I did. I didn't even know him."

"Close the door, please, and take a seat."

"Did you hear what I just said?"

"Yes, I heard you. Now, sit down."

Ginger wondered what crazy new theory he had cooked up. She sat down in front of his desk.

"We did a search of Susanna's car this morning and found something very interesting."

"You just got around to searching her car this morning? The killer could have planted something in it by now."

"Yes, that's true, but I know that this wasn't planted because Marilyn told me she saw Susanna put it in the console right before they drove here for the bake-off." He held up a sheet of pink paper and read from it. "Susanna, I've tried my best to be your friend, but you continue to hate me—which is fine. I can live with that. But today you were horribly disrespectful in a way that I didn't think even you were capable of. So, now the gloves are off. You are going down, Susanna Clampford. I will do everything in my power to ruin you and your bakery. You are dead. Not tomorrow. Maybe not next year, but eventually I will DESTROY you."

The chief looked up at her. "It's signed Ginger." He studied her face.

"What do you want me to say?"

"Did you write this?"

"It's not what you think."

"Oh, I don't know. It seems very clear to me."

"Look at the date. What's the date on it?"

He glanced at the note. "There is no date on it."

Ginger's heart sunk. "Chief, I wrote that years ago."

"You think that helps you? Looks to me like you did exactly what you told Susanna you were going to do. You said," he read from the note, "I will do everything in my power to ruin you and your bakery. You are dead. Not tomorrow. Maybe not next year, but eventually I will DESTROY you."

"But you don't know why Susanna brought that note with her. Maybe she wanted to clear the air. Maybe she was planning to burn it right in front of me and offer a truce. What did Marilyn say about it?"

"She asked Susanna why she was bringing it, but she never got a straight answer. However, it doesn't really matter what Susanna's intentions were. What matters is that you told her you were going to kill her."

"But, Chief—"

"Give me one good reason why I shouldn't book you right now."

"Because I didn't kill her."

"That's what they all say. You'll have to do better than that."

"Just give me a couple of weeks."

"I'll give you twenty-four hours."

"Twenty-four hours? No, that's not enough time."

"Okay, look, I'll give you until the end of the bake-off. As soon as the prizes have been awarded, the cuffs go on—unless I find a better suspect before then."

"I'll find you a better suspect, but I don't know if I can do it that fast."

"You promised that you'd leave the investigating up to me."

"That's not fair. It's my life and my freedom that's on the line."

"Okay, you're right. I'll make an exception this time. But if you dig up any clues, you've got to bring them to me immediately. Understand?"

"Yes, I understand."

Ginger left his office in a daze. She knew she must have looked drunk to the other people on the elevator. She walked out of the courthouse and sat down on a bench under a tree, took out her phone, and called Elijah.

He said, "Hey, sweetie. I missed you at breakfast. What happened? You never returned my text."

"Sorry, honey. I'm having a bad day."

"Have you had anything to eat?"

"No . . . I guess not."

"How about I grab a couple of sandwiches from Subway and pick you up? We'll have a picnic brunch."

"Sounds wonderful. I'm sitting on a bench in the courthouse yard, facing the bakery. I'll stay right here 'til you come."

"Be there in fifteen minutes."

CHAPTER TWENTY-SIX

Friday, 10:37 a.m.

*E*lijah pulled up in front of the courthouse, and Ginger got up from the bench and dragged herself to his car and got in.

"You look like you're starving." Elijah pulled away.

"My stomach's rumbling, but I don't feel hungry," Ginger said. "Probably because I still can't smell or taste anything. But I know I need to eat."

"Well, go ahead and start. You don't have to wait 'til we get there."

"Where are we going?"

"You'll see."

She reached into the Subway bag, took out a bag of potato chips, opened it, and popped a chip into her mouth. It tasted like a crispy piece of paper. No, not even that good. It had no flavor at all. "Thanks so much for rescuing me. I hope I didn't pull you away from something important."

"Nothing's more important than you."

"Aw, that's sweet."

"So, why are you having such a bad day?" He headed out of town.

"Because I thought I was getting somewhere with my investigation. Then the chief called me in and showed me a threatening note to Susanna that he found this morning."

"Well, a threatening note sounds like a solid clue."

"Yes, it does. Only problem is . . . I'm the one who wrote it. I said I was going to destroy her and her business—no matter how long it took."

"That doesn't sound like you at all."

"Six years ago, in the cemetery, right after Lester's graveside service, Susanna walked up to me and whispered in my ear, 'We reap what we sow,' as though Lester's premature death was God's payback for me stealing him away from Susanna in college all those years ago. She had this evil grin on her face. I'll never forget it."

"That was cruel."

"I couldn't stop thinking about it, and that night, when I was writing the note, I was so angry with her that I could barely see straight. I was out of my mind with rage. It made me physically ill. I drove it down to the post office and mailed it before I could change my mind. But, of course, the next morning I wished I hadn't mailed it."

"How did she respond?"

"She didn't. I never heard a thing from her. I figured she realized it was something I had done in the heat of the moment, so she just threw it away and forgot about it."

"But she didn't throw it away," he said. "She saved it."

"For six years."

He drove off the road onto the grass and parked. "Well, what do you think?"

"This is John Wilson's land, right? I mean, the land you bought from him. But the old house is gone. When did you do this?"

"Over the past month or so. A few of the deacons helped me tear it down, and I paid for the city to haul the mess away. Then I had the land cleared and treated for termites."

"Oh, that's right. The house was infested," she said. "Well, this is just beautiful. What a lovely piece of land."

"Two acres," he said. "Now I can start building our house."

"Our house?"

He reached into his jacket pocket and took out a small box.

Ginger felt her eyes widen. "Is that what I think it is?"

He laughed. "I considered hiding it in your sandwich, but I was afraid you might break a tooth."

"Oh, I can't do this."

"What do you mean?"

"I mean, I just can't. I'm not worthy. I'm a murder suspect, and I might even be guilty."

"No, you're not."

"I can't remember everything that happened."

"You didn't do it."

"There's no way you can know that—not for sure."

"Come on, sweetie. You're not a killer."

"Well, I'm definitely a liar."

"What are you talking about? I've never known you to lie about anything."

"I lie to the chief all the time—about where I've been, what I've been investigating. I'm a liar, and you're a pastor. You can't have a lying wife. That just won't work. No church wants a pastor with a liar for a wife. It just can't happen. And really, I've been thinking that I could never be a pastor's wife even if I wasn't a liar. I'm just not cut out for it. I'm not good enough."

"Okay, then. It's settled."

"What? That we won't get married?"

"No. That you won't be a pastor's wife."

"You're not making any sense, Elijah. Wait. Whoa, you're not quitting the ministry. Not because of me. No, no, no. I can't let you do that."

"I'm not quitting. I'm retiring."

"Retiring? Really?"

"Not right away. First, I need to build our house—and that'll take a while. Some of the men said they'd help, and as far as the materials, I'll pay as I go. Probably take a couple of years."

"So, you're talking about a long engagement."

He chuckled. "About two years, give or take."

"Oh. Wow." She thought for a moment. "But in the meantime, we'd be engaged, and the church members would expect me to start acting like a preacher's wife and—"

"Not a wife."

"Okay, a preacher's fiancée—which I can't do."

"Why not?"

"Because I don't know how to act like a preacher's fiancée. It wouldn't be long before I'd embarrass you."

"Okay," he said. "Let's just forget that I asked you to marry me."

Ginger felt her lower lip trembling, but she couldn't make it stop.

He put his hand on her shoulder. "I meant, let's just put it on hold for a while. At least until you're cleared of the murder."

"If I'm ever cleared. I could be going to prison. I just don't know."

He reached over and hugged her. "You're not going to prison. You're gonna be just fine."

CHAPTER TWENTY-SEVEN

Friday, 1:00 p.m.

*G*inger felt rejuvenated after her long lunch break, sitting in Elijah's car with the windows rolled down, breathing the country air, watching the squirrels, and listening to the birds. By the time he dropped her off at Coreyville Hotel, she was ready to roll. She had until three o'clock tomorrow, approximately twenty-six hours, to solve the case.

As soon as she walked into the lobby, her phone rang. It was Jane.

"I've got some information for you. It's a rumor, but it could be true."

"Great," Ginger said. "Just a second." She went out the back door of the lobby, through the cloud of cigarette smoke, and to the parking lot. "Okay, what have you got?"

"It's about Al Fenster. Back in 1985, he had a restaurant in Marshall, and it was doing really well. It had a bakery too."

"Yeah, I remember that, vaguely. So, what about it?"

"Well, apparently, he was starting to take customers away from Susanna's bakery, so she made an anonymous call to the health department, which led to a surprise inspection and ended up shutting down the restaurant for several days. After that, it was all downhill for Al, and he went out of business."

"Okay," Ginger said, "but if his place couldn't pass a health inspection, then it needed to be shut down."

"Yeah, but Al claimed that Susanna had hired a guy to go to work for him, and that the guy planted horse meat in his fridge to make it look like Al was substituting it for beef to increase profits."

"That's so dirty," Ginger said.

"Oh, it gets worse. The guy also threw some dead roaches into Al's flour right before the inspector came."

"Are you kidding me?"

"That's the claim," Jane said. "Now, he could have made it all up because he didn't want to take the blame for his own low standards."

"But it does sound like something Susanna might do."

Jane went on. "A few years later, Al got enough money together to open his deli and bakery in Longview, and it's done pretty well, although they say he's struggling to keep it afloat."

"If all this is true, you can certainly see why he would hate Susanna, but why would he wait until now to take revenge on her, after all these years?"

"I don't know," Jane said, "unless he thought it would be easier to get away with it now, since so much time has passed."

"Plus, there's the element of opportunity. They were both

staying overnight here in Coreyville, and several other bakery owners are here too. And most of them have a grudge against Susanna, judging by what I heard on that recording. Any of them could have done it, which is good for him."

"That's right," Jane said.

"Thank you for your help. I'm headed into the hotel right now, and I'm gonna find Al and have a little talk with him."

"Oh, wait—there's one more thing. Barb asked me to tell you that she called around in your neighborhood and nobody remembered seeing a black sports car on Wednesday night."

"If they'd seen that car, they definitely would have remembered it. Oh, well. It was worth a shot. Tell her thanks."

"I will. Good luck, Ginger."

She walked into the lobby. She would try the restaurant first since it was a little after one o'clock. Ginger spotted Al sitting in a booth alone, polishing off a piece of apple pie.

"What do think of the food here, Al?"

He quickly stuffed the remainder of the pie into his mouth. It was such a big piece that he couldn't possibly talk until he finished consuming it.

She sat down across from him and spoke softly. "You know, Al, I heard an interesting story about you and Susanna Clampford. How years ago she destroyed your restaurant in Marshall."

He began choking, grabbed his glass of water, and gulped it down.

"You okay?" she said.

He nodded.

"Is it true that she paid a mole to go to work for you and that he set you up for a bad health inspection?"

"Yeah, yeah. So what?"

"Didn't that make you want to strike back at her?"

"Absolutely. I can see where you're going with this, Ginger, so let me save you some time: I'm too much of a chicken to kill anybody, and that's all you need to know. I don't want to get into any further details about what she did to me back then because it makes me sick to my stomach, and I just ate. So, if you don't mind . . ."

"Okay."

"Look, Ginger, I know you're in a tough spot, and I really wish I could help you. Have you talked to Bobby Boudreaux?"

"Not yet."

"Well, I'm no rat, but did you know he was drunk Wednesday night, and that when he's drunk he gets angry and sometimes does crazy things that he doesn't remember?"

"How do you know that?"

"I'm surprised you didn't know. I thought everybody did."

"No, I've never heard this."

"Well, it's true, and when you talk to him, ask him why he was wearing the same clothes Thursday morning that he had on Wednesday night, and ask him where he was all night and what he was doing."

"So, you saw him walking around drunk?"

"We were in the bar together."

"What time was this?"

"He came in around eight, I guess, and he left a little after ten, I think. I was there 'til eleven-forty-five."

Ginger took out her phone and made note of the times Al had just given her. "Okay. Thanks for your help. And good luck in the contest."

"I'm going home with your first-place trophy this time."

Ginger smiled. "We'll see."

CHAPTER TWENTY-EIGHT

Friday, 1:28 p.m.

Ginger couldn't find Bobby Boudreaux in the restaurant or in his lesson partition, so she went up to his room.

When he opened the door and saw her, he looked nervous. "Ginger, what are you doing here?"

"Could I come in for a minute?"

"Uh, sure." He let her in and closed the door.

"What's going on?" he said.

"Where were you on Wednesday night when Susanna was murdered?"

"Whoa, really? You think I did it?"

"Were you drunk?"

"Who told you that?"

Ginger waited for an answer to her question.

He threw his hands in the air. "I don't know. I can't remember." He turned and walked away from her.

"Did you sleep in your clothes that night?"

He spun around. "Al Fenster told you that. Yes, I slept in my clothes. So what? That doesn't prove anything. I'm telling you, I couldn't have killed her. I could never do anything like that."

"But you can't remember what you did Wednesday night, so how can you be sure you didn't do it?"

"Because if I was going to kill Susanna Clampford, I would have done it a long time ago."

"Why? What do you mean?"

He studied her face. "You really don't know?"

"What?"

"Ever heard of Susanna's Big Boy Chocko Cake?"

"Of course. It's her best-seller."

"Yes! But it's my recipe!" He snatched up a suitcase by the handle and threw it across the room. It hit a nightstand and knocked off a lamp, breaking it.

Ginger stepped backward, toward the door, wondering if she should have brought her pepper spray. "Take it easy, Bobby. I understand you might have a similar recipe, but it couldn't be the one Susanna uses. That's been her most popular cake for years."

"I know! For eighteen years to be exact. That's when she stole it from me—while I was working for her. I was a freshman at ETBU. I tinkered with that recipe for months, and when I baked it up for Susanna, she said it was fantastic—that she'd never tasted anything like it. And right then and there I knew what I wanted to do with my life. She was so proud of me, and I was on top of the world. Then she stole the recipe and told everybody it was hers!"

"Why didn't you set the record straight right then?"

"Really, Ginger? Who do you think people were gonna believe: the bakery owner or some eighteen-year-old college kid? I was gonna use that recipe to kick off my own bakery. My dad would have probably loaned me the money for it if Susanna had given me the recommendation I was counting on."

"So, what did you do?"

"I dropped out of college and never went back and disappointed my father for the thousandth time. That's what I did."

"Well, this doesn't look good for you."

"So you're gonna run and tell the police?"

Ginger reached back and grasped the doorknob. "No. Not right now, anyway. I'm still gathering clues."

"Please don't tell them, Ginger. And think about it: why would I kill Susanna now? Doggers is doing great. Why would I do anything to screw it up?"

"I see what you're saying, Bobby. Thanks for your honesty."

She opened the door and quickly walked out.

CHAPTER TWENTY-NINE

Friday, 2:05 p.m.

Ginger wanted to believe Bobby Boudreaux—that he had nothing to do with the murder. She felt awful about the way Susanna had taken advantage of him when he was just a teenager—assuming his story was true. But Ginger wasn't totally convinced of his innocence. A cool-headed, rational man would certainly not want to jeopardize his successful business. But Bobby was certainly not cool-headed, and according to Al Fenster, he was completely irrational when drunk.

Al had said that Bobby had a history of getting angry and out of control when he drank too much, and Bobby had admitted to her that he wasn't sure where he went or what he did Wednesday while he was drunk.

Ginger wanted a second opinion on Bobby's apparent state of mind when he left the bar Wednesday night, so she went by the bar and questioned the bartender on duty to find out who had been working Wednesday night. It was Billy. Yes, she knew Billy. She looked up his address and went to his apartment. It was in town, within walking distance.

Billy came to the door wearing a T-shirt and what looked like pajama bottoms. He was barefoot, and his hair was matted and looked greasy.

"Oh, hi, Mrs. Lightley."

"Sorry to drop in on you like this, Billy, but I was wondering if I could ask you a few questions."

"You're investigating, aren't you? Well, I can save you some time. I was working Wednesday night at the time of the murder."

"Oh, I had no suspicions about you, but thanks for that," she said. "Mind if I come in for just a minute?"

"Sure." He let her in. There were empty beer cans on the coffee table and several piles of dirty clothes on the floor. "Excuse my mess. It's laundry day."

"No problem," she said. "So, on Wednesday night, two of the men who are participating in my bake-off were in the bar. I'm talking about Al Fenster and Bobby Boudreaux. Al's a big man—actually they're both big men—but Al's in his sixties and Bobby's in his thirties."

"Yeah, I remember them. What do you want to know?"

"Did they drink a lot?"

"Yes, ma'am, they did."

"Okay, so Bobby—the younger one—he left the bar first, right?"

"Yeah."

"Was he drunk when he left?"

"Oh, yeah. Definitely."

"Did he seem angry?"

"Yeah," he said. "He was going on about some woman who stole his cake recipe, saying that she was finally gonna pay."

"What else did he say?"

"That was mostly it. He just kept saying, 'She's gonna pay,' and he was cursing and calling her names. His face got bright red, and he was throwing such a fit I thought I was gonna have to call security. But then he left."

"Did you tell the police about this?"

"No. They haven't asked me anything."

"Hmm. What about the other man? Al. Was he angry too?"

"Didn't seem like it. I think he got a kick out of watching the other guy act all stupid."

"Did either one of them say anything else that you think I might want to know about?"

"Not really."

"Do you remember what time the two of them came into the bar?"

"Uh . . . Al came in around eight or eight-thirty, and the other guy, Bobby, came in around nine or so."

"About what time did he leave?"

"I'd guess somewhere between ten and ten-thirty."

"Okay, Billy. Thanks for your help."

"Don't you want to know about Al—what time he left?"

"I think I already know," she said. "Eleven-forty-five, right?"

"Well, yeah, that's about when he closed out his tab, but he wasn't there the whole time."

"Wait. You're saying that he left and came back?"

"Yeah. He was gone at least forty-five minutes, I'd say—maybe an hour."

"And this was after Bobby left—so between ten-thirty and eleven-forty-five?"

"Yeah, something like that."

"Thanks, Billy. You've been very helpful."

CHAPTER THIRTY

Friday, 4:02 p.m.

Ginger waited at the back of Al Fenster's training partition until he released his class and they cleared out. She walked in as he was about to leave. He didn't look thrilled to see her.

"How did your session go, Al?"

"Fine. Everybody really enjoyed it."

"Good."

"But that's not why you're here, is it?"

"I have a couple more questions."

"Shoot."

Her phone started ringing. It was Elijah calling. She silenced it. "So, I talked to the bartender who was on duty Wednesday night—"

"And he told you I left the bar for a while—at the exact time the murder took place?"

"Basically. So where'd you go?"

"I told Maybelle that I've been working out every day. She wants me to lose some weight—you know, for health reasons." A look of terror came over his face. "Oh, did you know about me and Maybelle?"

Ginger smiled. "I think everybody knows about you two, Al."

"Really? Well, do me a favor and don't tell Maybelle that."

"I won't."

"Anyway, Wednesday night after Bobby left the bar, I realized I hadn't hit the gym that day, so that's where I went."

"You went to the hotel gym and worked out—even though you'd been drinking heavily?"

"Yeah. I know it's crazy, but I promised her I'd go every day, so I had to go in for a while and do something."

"How long were you in the gym?"

"Forty-five minutes or so."

"Well, that explains it. Thanks, Al."

"And remember, don't tell Maybelle that everybody knows we're dating. And whatever you do, don't tell her daughter, Caroline."

"I won't say a word about it."

She walked out to the lobby and checked her phone. Elijah had not left a voicemail, so she called him back.

He said, "You want to meet for dinner?"

"This is getting to be a habit, sir. And isn't it sort of early for dinner?"

"I need to be at the funeral home by six for a viewing."

"Oh, that's right. You told me that at lunch."

"I'm sure you wouldn't be interested in coming to the funeral home. You didn't even know Mr. Johnston, and besides, you're working the case."

"I'm trying to."

"But you've got to eat."

"I still don't have any appetite, but yeah, I should eat."

"How about Bull Crawley's? His chicken fried chicken is so good that it just might bring your taste buds back to life."

"I'd try anything if I thought it could do that."

"How's four-thirty?"

"There's something I need to check on first. Is four-forty-five okay?"

"Sure."

Ginger didn't believe Al's story about going to the gym for forty-five minutes on Wednesday night. Trying to work out after drinking all that liquor? She tracked down the hotel manager and asked for his help. Together, they scanned the surveillance recording from the gym cameras between nine and eleven-forty-five on Wednesday night.

Al Fenster never came into the gym.

CHAPTER THIRTY-ONE

Friday, 6:15 p.m.

Ginger and Elijah ate dinner at Bull Crawley's Restaurant & Grill. She was still not able to smell or taste anything, but she did enjoy Elijah's company. Afterwards, he'd dropped her off at the carnival and headed to the funeral home to comfort the bereaved family.

She was on her way to see Al Fenster, who had lied regarding his whereabouts—twice. First, he'd said he was sitting in the bar until eleven-forty-five. Then he'd told her he'd left the bar and gone to the hotel gym for forty-five minutes to an hour. Another lie. Ginger couldn't wait to confront him.

She walked up to Al's tent. He and his two workers were helping several customers with their purchases of cakes, muffins, and cinnamon rolls. She tried to get his attention, but he ignored her. Finally, she shouted, "You lied to me, Al Fenster."

Everyone in line looked back at Ginger. Al motioned for her to meet him behind the tent. She walked around to the back and he came out.

"Are you trying to scare my customers away?"

"You lied to me about going to the gym."

"No, I didn't."

"Yes, you did. They've got a couple of cameras in the gym, and the hotel manager showed me the surveillance footage."

"Okay, yeah, yeah, I lied because I didn't want you to tell Maybelle what I was doing."

Ginger's eyebrows shot up. "Committing murder?"

"No, no. I went out back in the parking lot to smoke."

"For forty-five minutes?"

"It was a cigar, okay. Please don't tell Maybelle. I've been trying to quit. Honestly."

Ginger shook her head.

"It's the truth. I promise you."

"I'm supposed to believe you now, after you've already lied to me twice?"

"I know. You've got every right to be mad at me. I'm sorry, but please don't tell Maybelle. Okay?"

Ginger just stared at him.

He went back into his tent and Ginger walked away.

She was headed to her bakery's tent when Caroline Rogers walked up to her. She looked perturbed. "Can I talk to you for a minute?"

"Sure."

"I know you're investigating the murder, and I don't blame you. That ridiculous police chief seems to think you're the killer—which is preposterous, of course, but I want you to stay away from my mother. She told me you interrogated her this morning and—"

"Interrogated her? Not at all. I just asked her a few questions, and—"

"Well, you just leave her alone. Understand?"

Why was Caroline so upset about Ginger quizzing Maybelle? What were the two of them hiding that she was afraid her mother might accidentally give away?

Caroline's left eye was twitching ever so slightly.

"Yes," Ginger said. "I understand."

"Good. And by the way, I checked into the hotel at one-fifteen a.m. Wednesday night, and when I got off the elevator to go to my room, I spotted Fredrick Marcello going into Kate Lake's room. I didn't realize it was her room until the next day, but I think those two were up to something. They're supposed to be bitter enemies, aren't they? Seemed awfully fishy to me." She turned and marched away.

Ginger walked to Fredrick's tent. His workers were busy serving customers. Fredrick was shuffling some boxes around in the back of the tent. Ginger went to the back and was about to peek in when she heard one of Fredrick's workers talking to him.

"Mr. Marcello, that guy from the bank is still calling every day."

"What did you say to him?"

"I said exactly what you told me to say: that you're out of the country this week and that you can't be reached by phone."

"Good, good."

"But he said they're gonna come pick up your car."

"It's okay, Blake. I'll handle it next week."

Ginger waited twenty seconds and then poked her head in. "Fredrick?"

He jumped. "Oh, Ginger, honey, you nearly made me pee my pants."

"Sorry about that, but I need to talk to you. It's urgent."

He came outside.

"Are you okay?" she asked.

"Yeah, yeah, sure."

"Okay, I've got to confess that I overheard your conversation with your employee."

"Huh?"

"Just a minute ago," she said. "Are you in financial trouble? Is there anything I can do to help?"

"No, I just . . . I'm gonna have to sell my car."

"Oh, I'm sorry. I know how much you love it. Is this because you've been helping Kate start up her bakery?"

"What? No."

"Okay. Well, the reason I'm here is to ask you what you and Kate were doing together on Wednesday night."

"Oh, Miss Ginger, Kate broke up with me six months ago. She won't have anything to do with me."

"Then why were you in her hotel room?"

He hesitated. "How did you know about that?"

"I have eyes and ears everywhere." Oh, how she wished it were true. "Now be straight with me."

"I'm still in love with her."

"I already knew that. What I want to know is exactly what you were doing in her room."

"Well, I . . ."

"The two of you killed Susanna."

"What? No way. No, we had nothing to do with that."

"I think you came to my house Wednesday night to set me up—to make sure I was there at home and awake when Susanna's fake phone call came in. That was really Kate calling, wasn't it?"

"No."

"Tell me the truth, Fredrick."

"I mean, she told me we needed to stick with the plan, and I kind of thought she was talking about the murder plan, you know, like a joke thing, whatever, and I just wanted to make her happy, so I went to your house. But later, I found out she was really talking about the plan we made about our big public breakup and pretending that we hated each other and all that. It had nothing to do with the murder."

"Your breakup was a publicity stunt?"

"Yes, but don't tell anybody. It was to kick-start her bakery. You know how hard it is to get customers when you open a new business, Ginger. Anyway, it worked."

"Unbelievable." Ginger walked away.

"But, wait, Miss Ginger. Come back. We didn't do anything wrong."

Fredrick was gullible, but probably innocent.

She wasn't so sure about Kate.

CHAPTER THIRTY-TWO

Friday, 6:30 p.m.

*G*inger was walking back to her bakery's tent when Joey Joffs appeared out of nowhere and nearly bumped into her. Joey was a butcher by day, a drunk by night. Amazingly, he still had all ten fingers.

"Hey, there, Mrs. Ginger O'Lightley."

She had given up trying to correct him. Thankfully, Joey didn't turn mean when he got drunk. He turned sort of Irish.

"Hello, Joey."

He leaned in. "I've got some vital information for you, Mrs. O'Lightley."

His breath was a fire hazard.

"Information about the murder?"

He leaned in closer. "Shh! I seen the lass with me own two eyes."

"Who?"

"The lovely one with the long, brownish curls. I saw her

coming out of the cemetery on the night of the bloody murder. There, in that tent." He pointed to the tent of Susanna's Cakery.

Ginger saw Marilyn, with her long brown hair, chatting with a customer, smiling sweetly. This was vital information—if it turned out to be true. "Are you sure it was—"

He was gone. Lost in the crowd. It was just as well. Joey was probably the least reliable witness in town. But she still needed to check it out. Both Marilyn and Al had said they were in the hotel parking lot at the time of the murder. Marilyn in Susanna's car, playing a game on her phone, and Al, standing around smoking a cigar.

Marilyn had told her that when she walked out the back door of the lobby Wednesday night to go to Susanna's car, several smokers had seen her. Ginger remembered that earlier in the day she too had walked past smokers who were sitting outside that door. She wondered if any of them would remember seeing Marilyn or Al on Wednesday night.

Ginger walked to the hotel, went through the lobby to the back door, and walked outside. Sure enough, there were five hotel employees sitting around talking, laughing, and smoking. Two women and three men.

"Excuse me," Ginger said, "do you mind if I ask y'all a few questions? It's about Wednesday night."

"You're Ginger Lightly," one of the women said.

"Yes, I am."

"Is this about the murder?"

"Yeah. Were all of y'all working Wednesday night?"

They all said they were.

"Did any of you see this man go in or out of this door?" She held out her phone and showed them Al Fenster's picture.

One of the women said, "Yeah, he was that big, fat guy. He lit up a cigar and walked out into the parking lot somewhere."

"Do you remember what time it was?" Ginger asked.

One of the men said, "It was right before the end of my break at ten-fifteen."

The woman agreed.

"Did anybody see him go back inside?"

None of them had.

"How about this woman?" Ginger showed them a picture of Marilyn.

"Whoa, man, she's hot!" one of the men said.

"Yeah, I remember her," another man said. "It was during my lunch break. She walked out to the parking lot and got into a car."

Another man said, "Yeah, but she didn't go anywhere."

"It was around nine-thirty-five," the first man said.

"Yeah, that's about right," the second man said.

"Did anybody see her go back into the hotel?" Ginger asked.

"Yeah, I did," one of the women said. "Around eleven-fifteen. I had just started my break when she walked in."

"Yeah," one of the men said. "But then I saw her go in again, like ten minutes later."

The woman said, "What? I didn't see that."

"Yeah," he said, "she must have gone out the front and walked back around here."

The woman said, "He doesn't know what he's talking about."

"I'm telling you, that's what I saw," he said.

"Okay," Ginger said, "how about this woman?" She showed them Kate's picture.

"Wow, another hottie," one man said.

"So did anybody see her go in or out of this door on Wednesday night?"

They all said they hadn't.

She showed them pictures of Bobby, Maybelle, and Caroline. None of the smokers had seen any of them on Wednesday night. Ginger thanked them for their help, walked into the lobby, and plopped herself down in a chair.

Her investigation was going nowhere.

CHAPTER THIRTY-THREE

Friday, 8:20 p.m.

*G*inger sat in the hotel lobby for over an hour. Her mind was spinning. Tomorrow was Saturday, the day of the cake contest, and after that, all of Ginger's contestants would be leaving Coreyville and heading home to Marshall, Longview, Tyler, or Gladewater, making it more difficult for her—and the chief—to question them. And if the chief arrested her right after the contest, as he planned, her investigation activities would end immediately.

Ginger couldn't defend herself adequately because of her memory loss. She couldn't state with full confidence exactly what happened Wednesday night in the cemetery, so how would she ever convince the chief—or a jury? And how would she even know when she had regained all of her memories? There was nobody else—except the killer—who knew what really happened out there.

Her phone rang and she took it out. There was no name, just a number, but it looked familiar.

"Hello?"

"Ginger, this Judy Jo Bailey. How's the investigation going? Have you tracked down the killer yet?"

"No, I'm afraid not, and I'm still the chief's prime suspect."

"Well, I think I have something that will help you."

"What is it?"

"I know you didn't find any evidence yesterday against Marilyn, and that you think I'm wrong about her having an affair with Chuck, but I'm here at the office building where Chuck taught private music lessons, and I've been talking to the guy who cleans the building every week. He does it at night, like from nine to one in the morning when everybody's gone, and when I told him I was particularly interested in Chuck Clampford's office, he said that Chuck was usually the last tenant to leave at night, and—"

"But Chuck died two months ago," Ginger said.

"I know, but this guy says Chuck's stuff is still in his office, and his name is still on the door."

"How weird."

"And, he told me that sometimes Chuck would be here 'til midnight, and that he'd seen several older women coming out of his office at eleven o'clock or later."

"Wonder what he means by older women," Ginger said. "How old is this guy?"

"Early twenties."

"Yeah, so his idea of an older woman is probably forty, and Marilyn is mid-forties."

"Right, and get this: he told me that one time he had to skip cleaning Chuck's office altogether because he was still in there with some woman at one o'clock in the morning. So, I showed him a picture of Marilyn and asked him if he'd ever seen her. He seemed to recognize her, but he told me that if I wanted more information I'd have to pay."

"Well, go ahead and pay him, and I'll pay you back."

"I can't, Ginger. He wants five hundred dollars."

"Five hundred dollars! That's ridiculous."

"I know, and I don't have that much anyway. I'm paycheck to paycheck. I guess I blew it by sounding too eager."

"No, don't feel bad about it."

"But I really think this guy knows something. I mean, if he can say for sure that he saw Marilyn up here late at night with Chuck . . ."

This was nuts. Was Ginger really going to drive to Marshall tonight and pay some guy five hundred dollars in the slim hope that he might have a solid clue? Was she that desperate?

Ginger pictured herself sitting in jail, awaiting trial.

"Will you stick around and wait for me?" Ginger asked.

"Sure. I'll text you the address. Oh, and he said it has to be cash."

"Of course. I'll be there as quick as I can."

She called Addie and told her what she was about to do. Addie questioned her mental state, but Ginger assured her that she was fine and that she'd be careful.

She walked to her house, got into her car, and drove to the ATM machine at her bank. She withdrew five hundred dollars but hoped she wouldn't have to use it all. Maybe she could talk the guy down.

As she was driving out of town, she noticed that a black SUV seemed to be following her. It stayed behind her all the way to Marshall. A couple of times she slowed down, hoping it would pass her, but it never did.

Ginger grew more tense with each mile.

CHAPTER THIRTY-FOUR

Friday, 9:10 p.m.

When Ginger turned onto the 390 Loop in Marshall, the black SUV that had followed her all the way from Coreyville stayed on her tail. What was going to happen when she reached the office building where Judy Jo was waiting?

Ginger pictured it: she steps out of her car, the SUV pulls up, a window rolls down, and an AK-47 riddles her with bullets.

Too much TV. She shouldn't have even known what an AK-47 was.

When she exited the loop, the other car did not, and she breathed a sigh of relief. She pulled into the parking lot of the three-story office building. There were only two cars in the entire lot, parked close to the main entrance. Judy Jo was standing by one of them. Ginger parked beside her car and got out.

Judy Jo said, "I know you must think I'm crazy, but I just kept thinking about how you didn't find any evidence of Chuck being in Marilyn's apartment, and I wondered if they might have been getting together here in his music studio instead."

"So, you came down here and started nosing around. You're turning into Nancy Drew."

She smiled. "Or Ginger Lightley."

"I don't know. Right now I feel like I'm just bumbling around in the dark hoping to get lucky." They went into the building.

"I hear a vacuum cleaner," Ginger said.

"That's him. Sounds like he's here on the first floor—which is perfect because Chuck's studio's on this floor."

They walked halfway down the hall and found Jake vacuuming a large office suite. He was a short, wimpy-looking guy.

Judy Jo tried to get his attention. "Hey, Jake. Hello?"

He noticed them and turned off the vacuum. "Got the cash?"

Ginger said, "I've got the cash if you've got the information I want."

He walked over to Ginger. "Five hundred dollars, cash."

"I'm not giving you a dime until you tell me what you know."

"Sorry, lady. If you want the dirt on Chuck Clampford, then you'll have to cough up the full five hundred."

"That's too much," Ginger said.

"That's my price. Take it or leave it."

Ginger looked at Judy Jo and shook her head. She reached into her pocket and took out the wad of twenty-dollar bills. "This better be worth it, or I'm gonna wrap that vacuum cleaner hose around your neck and strangle you with it." She couldn't believe she'd said it out loud.

Judy Jo looked surprised, but proud.

"That won't be necessary." He took the cash.

"Spill," Judy Jo said.

"Okay. So, one night, a few months ago, I was cleaning his office, and I found a condom wrapper under his couch."

"He's got a couch in his office?" Ginger said.

"Yeah. A big one."

"Did you see a woman leaving his office that night?"

"No, but I did see him leaving around midnight. I did his office last."

"How does that help us?" Ginger asked.

"I don't know. That's your problem."

"That's all you've got?" Judy Jo asked.

"Like I said, I didn't see her—but I smelled her perfume in his office. It was nice." He grinned.

"What fragrance was it?" Ginger asked.

He shrugged. "I don't know."

Judy Jo held up her phone to show him a picture of Marilyn. "Did you ever see this woman going in or out of Chuck's office?"

"Yeah."

"About how many times?" Ginger asked.

"I don't know," he said. "A couple, I guess."

"You guess?" Judy Jo said.

"I want to see Chuck's office," Ginger said.

"I'm sorry, but I'm not allowed to let anyone into the offices."

Judy Jo yelled, "Where do you think we are right now?"

"Yeah, but I didn't let you into this office—you just walked in."

Ginger said, "Well, then go unlock Chuck's office and we'll just walk in there."

"I could get fired for that."

"This is crap!" Judy Jo said.

Ginger raised her voice. "You could get fired if I tell your boss you're shaking down people for information about his tenants."

"Okay, okay," he said. "Come on." He led them to the end of the hallway. The sign on the door read *Chuck Clampford, Private Music Instruction.*

Jake unlocked the door, and they went in. There was a long red sofa on one wall, a studio piano on another, a desk, a table with a mini fridge on top of it, a couple of chairs, and a private bathroom.

Judy Jo said, "I think I smell perfume."

"What is it?" Ginger asked. "My nose still isn't working."

Judy Jo leaned over the couch. "Yeah . . . I know this from somewhere."

"Come on, you can do it," Ginger said. "Sniff it out."

Judy Jo got down on her knees and sniffed all over the couch like a dog. "Oh! I've got it! It's what my grandmother wears: Chanel No. 5."

"Are you sure?" Ginger asked. "Because it could be important."

Judy Jo smiled. "Yes, that's what it is."

"Great. Thanks for being my nose."

"What's wrong with your nose?" Jake asked.

"None of your business," Judy Jo said.

Ginger went to the desk and began looking through the drawers. They were all empty.

Judy Jo checked the closet and the bathroom.

"You shouldn't be touching everything," he said.

"Nobody will care, believe me," Ginger said. "The police already finished their investigation."

"They thought he might have been murdered, right?" Jake asked.

"Yes," Ginger said, "but they ended up ruling it an accident."

"The closet and the bathroom are empty." Judy Jo checked the mini fridge and the piano bench.

"There's nothing in the desk either," Ginger said.

Judy Jo said, "The cops took everything, I guess. I wonder if they found his appointment book."

"Yeah, they did," Ginger said. "He kept it in his phone, according to Dot Harbington. But the names were in some weird code, and the police never could figure out what they were."

"So, nobody knows who his students were?" Judy Jo asked.

"You'd think that some of them would have come forward to help with the investigation," Ginger said.

"Unless they were all lovers," Judy Jo said.

"Whoa. Way to go, dude," Jake said.

"You're gross," Judy Jo said.

Ginger took out her phone, went to a website, and showed Jake a picture. "How about this woman? Ever seen her?"

"Oh, yeah," Jake said, "I definitely remember her. I walked out of an office into the hallway one night and she nearly ran over me. You should have seen the look on her face. I thought she was gonna rip my head off. I don't know what her problem was."

"Who is it, Ginger?" Judy Jo asked.

Ginger showed her the picture. "Caroline Rogers."

"So, are we done here?" Jake asked.

"Yes," Ginger said. "But I expect you to keep your mouth shut for that five hundred dollars. We were never here. Understand?"

"Got it," he said. "No problem."

Ginger and Judy Jo left the building and walked out to their cars.

Judy Jo said, "I remember Caroline Rogers from the bake-off last year. Is she one of your suspects?"

"She is now. When I questioned her mother, Maybelle, about Caroline this morning, she told me that her daughter was taking piano lessons from a teacher here in Marshall—the same woman who taught her when she was a child. So I called the woman and found out that she retired from teaching over six months ago."

"But Maybelle said she was still taking lessons from the woman?" Judy Jo asked.

"Yes, but she squirmed a little when I asked her for the teacher's name."

"Maybe her old teacher recommended a new one," Judy Jo said.

"Yeah, and maybe it was Chuck Clampford. Of course, even if she was taking lessons from Chuck, it doesn't mean she started having an affair with him. That's a stretch."

"But it's possible, and doesn't it make you wonder if that's why Caroline's mother acted funny when you asked for the teacher's name?" Judy Jo asked.

"Yes, it does, and I'm gonna . . ."

"What?"

"I've got a flat tire. Look." Ginger showed her the front driver's side tire.

"You must have run over a nail or something," Judy Jo said.

Ginger looked around. "Or maybe somebody stabbed it with an ice pick."

"What makes you say that?"

"There was a black SUV following me all the way from Coreyville," Ginger said. "Of course, it was probably nothing. I'm feeling a little paranoid right now. Like you said, I probably just ran over a nail." Ginger took out her phone. "I'm calling Triple-A. They'll come and put the spare on for me."

"I'll stay with you 'til they're done."

"Thanks."

CHAPTER THIRTY-FIVE

Friday, 9:55 p.m.

On her way back to Coreyville, Ginger called Addie and asked her if they needed her help to shut things down for the night. Addie told her no, and that she should go straight to Ginger Bread House and get a good night's sleep.

When she arrived at Ginger Bread House, she slipped into the office, avoiding the guests. The room was dimly lit. A single lamp near the door was the only light in the large room, but Ginger didn't bother to turn on the overheads or any of the other lamps.

She went to her chair and sat in the darkness with her thoughts, staring through the windows in front of her, mesmerized by a ghostly mix of images: the tall pine trees in the front yard, weirdly accentuated by the landscape lighting, blended with her own reflection. She saw herself sitting on a throne atop the trees, looking down with a somber expression. In a trance, mulling the inevitable. By tomorrow at this time, she would be sitting in jail. She tried to concentrate on the clues she had collected and make sense of them, but her mind was mush. She just couldn't . . .

The overhead lights came on, blinding her.

"Ready for bed?" Ethel walked up to her chair holding two cups of cocoa.

"Uh, no, I was just resting my eyes."

Ethel handed her a cup of cocoa. "Well, this may put you back to sleep."

"It better not." Barb walked up carrying her own cup of cocoa.

Jane was right behind her. "Yeah, because we want to hear the latest."

The three sat down in their chairs.

Ginger took a sniff of the cocoa. "Hey, I can smell it!"

"Wonderful!" Jane said.

"That's great!" Barb said.

"It smells like mud," Ginger said.

"That's not nice," Ethel said. "I made it like I always do."

"It's not you, Ethel. It's me," Ginger said. "My smeller is still out of whack."

"But at least it's alive," Barb said.

"Yeah," Jane said.

Ginger smelled her arm. "Ew. My skin smells like —never mind."

"How about your taster?" Ethel asked. "Try the cocoa."

Ginger sipped it. "It tastes like mud too—which is progress, I know. I should be thankful, and I am, but unless I'm back one hundred percent by tomorrow, I won't be able to do my Sniff-Out."

"It wouldn't be the end of the world," Jane said. "The important thing is that you're getting better."

"I know," Ginger said.

"So, how's your investigation going?" Ethel asked. "We need details."

"Sure, okay. I've got some new clues," Ginger said. "But unfortunately, the strongest one points to me."

"Oh, no," Jane said.

"The chief found a note in Susanna's car. He and his brainy deputies just thought to search it this morning."

"Typical," Barb said. "What kind of note?"

"It was from me, telling Susanna I was going to kill her."

"Well, isn't that convenient?" Jane asked. "Obviously, the killer wrote it himself and planted it in her car."

"Yeah," Ethel said. "Doesn't the chief have enough brains to know it's a fake?"

"Problem is," Ginger said, "it's not fake."

Barb sat up straight. "Huh?"

"What are you talking about, girl?" Jane asked.

"I wrote it," Ginger said.

"Wait, I'm confused," Jane said. "Why would you write a note to Susanna saying you were gonna kill her?"

"It was six years ago, and I wrote it in the heat of the moment."

"So, you didn't really mean it," Barb said. "It was an exaggeration, right? You didn't literally plan to kill her."

"To be honest, I kind of did," Ginger said. "At the moment I wrote that note, I literally wanted to kill her."

"I can't imagine what would have made you feel so violent like that," Jane said.

"Yeah, that's just not like you," Ethel said.

"It was the day of Lester's funeral," Ginger said. "Susanna came. Remember?"

"Yeah, I remember," Barb said. "We were all shocked when she showed up."

"I had no idea that her coming had upset you so much," Jane said. "You never said anything."

"It wasn't the fact that she came," Ginger said. "I mean, she'd been in love with Lester at one time, so I had no problem with her coming to the funeral. I gave her the benefit of the doubt, thinking that she had finally dropped her grudge against me. But, of course, she wasn't over it. At the cemetery, after the service, she came up and whispered something in my ear . . ." Ginger clinched her jaw, "that I will never, ever forget."

"What did she say?" Jane asked.

"She said we reap what we sow—as though Lester's premature death was God's way of punishing me for stealing Lester away from her forty years ago."

"You're kidding?" Barb said. "She actually said that? I always knew Susanna Clampford was nothing but trailer trash."

"Easy, Barb," Jane said. "The woman's dead."

"Oh, that's just horrible that she would say something like that," Ethel said.

"No wonder you sent her a nasty note," Jane said.

"At first, I was hurt," Ginger said. "I even thought maybe she was right. But by that night, I was hopping mad, so I fired off the note and took it to the post office. The next day, I wished I hadn't mailed it."

"Exactly what did you say in the note?" Jane said.

"That she had been horribly disrespectful, and that I was

gonna do everything in my power to destroy her and her business."

"Wow, that's pretty strong," Jane said.

Ginger went on. "And that sooner or later, I was going to kill her."

"Oh, boy," Barb said.

"To tell you the truth, I had forgotten how vicious I sounded in the note," Ginger said.

"But, you'd think Susanna would have thrown it away long ago," Jane said.

"Maybe that's why she was walking over to my house to talk to me Wednesday night."

"To finally make a truce," Ethel said.

"Or to get into a fist fight," Barb said.

"Either way, it makes me partly responsible for her death," Ginger said.

"Don't you dare let anybody hear you talking like that," Jane said. "Especially the chief."

"You said you had other clues," Barb said.

"Yeah, several," Ginger said. "Some of them are probably red herrings, though. I got a call tonight from Judy Jo Bailey in Marshall."

"She's the college student who loaned you the key to Marilyn Monastrovi's apartment."

"Right," Ginger said. "So, long story short, I drove down to Marshall and—"

"Tonight?" Ethel said.

"Yes," Ginger said. "Got there around nine, and we talked to the guy who cleans the office building where Chuck Clampford taught private music lessons."

"But he died two months ago," Barb said.

"Yeah," Ginger said, "so you'd think his office would have been leased out to somebody else by now. But Susanna hadn't done a thing with it. His name was still on the door, and his piano and desk were still in there, along with a full-size sofa."

"A sofa?" Jane asked. "Why did he need a sofa to teach music lessons?"

"The cleaning guy found a condom wrapper under it a few months ago," Ginger said.

Jane chuckled. "Okay, so that's why he needed it."

"And that bit of information may be relevant." Ginger told them about Maybelle and Caroline and the piano lessons.

"So, Caroline was having an affair with Chuck," Ethel said, "and Susanna found out about it somehow, so she murdered Chuck and made it look like an accident, but Caroline was in love with Chuck and she didn't believe his death was an accident, and she figured Susanna had murdered him, so she killed Susanna with your shovel in the cemetery the other night."

"Well," Barb said, "that was one heck of a mouthful."

Jane looked at Ginger. "But that's what you're thinking, isn't it?"

"It's a possibility," Ginger said. "But of course, it's all conjecture. I can't prove anything."

Barb said, "So, why would Maybelle tell you that Caroline's been taking piano lessons in Marshall, knowing you might figure out that she had been involved with Chuck Clampford?"

"She didn't know," Jane said. "Maybelle didn't know her daughter had become involved with him, and that Caroline might be the one who killed Susanna. That's the only explanation. Maybelle didn't know."

"Maybe she didn't know that Caroline might have murdered Susanna," Ginger said, "but I do think she knew that her daughter was lying to her about something. And then there's Marilyn Monastrovi. She might have also visited Chuck in his studio. The cleaning guy thought he'd seen her there a couple of times."

"So, Marilyn could have been Chuck's lover and the one who killed Susanna," Jane said.

"It's enough to give you a migraine," Ethel said.

"And there's more." Ginger told them about Bobby drinking too much Wednesday night and not remembering what he did that night, and how Al lied to her twice about where he was at the time of the murder. Then she told them about the suspicious rendezvous between Fredrick and Kate.

By the time they finished discussing it all, they still didn't know for sure who killed Susanna or who attacked Ginger, or whether Chuck was murdered, and if so, by whom.

Jane, Barb, and Ethel went to bed. Ginger told them she wanted to sit up and ponder the clues for a bit longer. Jane begged her not to stay up too late.

CHAPTER THIRTY-SIX

Saturday, 12:41 a.m.

The girls had been in bed for nearly an hour. Jane had turned off the overhead lights, leaving on only the lamp near Ginger's chair and the one by the door. Obviously, she'd hoped the dim lighting would ease Ginger into a sleepy state. But that wasn't going to happen. Ginger felt reinvigorated by the fact that her senses of smell and taste were returning. She sniffed her arm again. It still didn't smell quite right, but it was getting closer by the minute.

Ginger vowed to never again complain that certain fragrances gave her a headache because they were too pungent for her sensitive nose. She yearned for that glorious pain.

She had a list of seven suspects, with only fourteen hours left to solve the murder. Maybe her nightmare of the chief and his deputies breaking down her door and hauling her off to jail wasn't a dream, but a premonition. Her destiny.

No. She would not give up. Think, Ginger. Figure it out.

Marilyn Monastrovi had said she was in Susanna's car, playing a game on her phone at the time of the murder. Fredrick Marcello had just left Ginger's house, alone. Kate Lake was supposedly alone in her hotel room. Al Fenster said he was alone in the hotel parking lot smoking a cigar. Maybelle Rogers said she was alone in her hotel room. Caroline Rogers said she was alone in Maybelle's Bakery in Tyler. Bobby Boudreaux was reportedly drunk, and said he couldn't remember where he was or what he was doing.

Every one of them appeared to have a motive except for Maybelle. However, she could have been involved in the murder because of her relationship with Al or Caroline. She certainly seemed to be hiding something.

There was also the possibility that the killer was somebody other than one of her seven suspects. Ginger didn't even want to think about that.

If only her memories of Wednesday night would clear up. Maybe going back to the scene of the crime would spur her memory. Ginger never had a chance to inspect the crime scene. Wednesday night when she came to, she'd been too sick to her stomach to get up and look around. Then the paramedics carried her away. The area was probably still taped off, but nobody would know if she went out there in the middle of the night.

She found a heavy-duty flashlight in one of the cabinets and turned it on. The batteries seemed strong, but she replaced them with new ones anyway. Ginger wasn't going to take a chance this time. She put on her coat and quietly slipped out to her car. She hoped she wouldn't wake up anyone when she started the engine. If one of the girls did wake up, she'd know about it right away because they would be calling her cell and asking where the heck she was going at this time of night.

Ginger started her car and creeped down the long driveway to the road. She drove to her house and parked. Her phone hadn't rung, so she was confident that she hadn't woken up the girls while sneaking away.

She got out of her car, walked around to the back yard, and was about to open the gate to the cemetery when she remembered she still hadn't oiled the hinges. She knew they were going to squeal. When she'd opened the gate Wednesday night, she'd been lucky. Her neighbor had not woken up. Although if the gate noise had roused Mrs. Martin and she'd called in the cops, and if they would have arrived in time to scare off the killer, then Ginger wouldn't have been attacked and Susanna might be alive.

Too many ifs.

She went to her house, unlocked the back door, went into her kitchen, and got a can of WD-40 from under the sink. Then she went back out to the gate, sprayed the hinges, and set the can near the fence. As she slowly opened the gate to the cemetery, her mind flashed back to Wednesday night, standing in that same spot wearing no coat in forty-something-degree weather, about to walk into an ambush.

Ginger followed the trail and was nearly to her gravestone when she came upon the crime scene tape. She ducked under it, and went to her gravestone and inspected it.

The chief was right: there was no date of death on her gravestone. Yet she remembered so clearly how shocked she'd been when she saw it. Her memories were still playing tricks on her.

She knelt down and ran her hand across the surface of the

lower part of the gravestone where she thought she'd seen the date of death. It was smooth. Of course it was. It would have been impossible to carve into the stone and then patch it to its original glassy-smooth state. Then she felt something slightly sticky. She located four tiny sticky spots.

Her memories weren't wrong! Somebody had covered the lower part of her gravestone with a sheet of paper that looked similar to the rest of the carved stone, with the date of death on it. No, no, it was probably transparency film—the stuff they use with overhead projectors.

But why did they do it? To get her attention. To cause her to lean down for a closer look, putting her in a vulnerable position, so they could hit her over the head with the shovel.

Ginger pointed her flashlight down at the grassy area in front of her gravestone and felt it with her hand. If her memories were correct, she might be able to find an indentation where the back end of a flashlight was jammed into the ground to shine the light up toward her gravestone.

She found it! She was right about the flashlight too!

Her memories had been accurate: the flashlight and the date of death she remembered seeing on her gravestone had been there. The ER doctor had told her that she might suffer temporary memory loss. And she had. When she regained consciousness in the cemetery, she was having trouble remembering things, but by the time the chief came to question her in the ER, her memory problems had probably already cleared up. She had thought so—until the chief told her that there was no date of death on her gravestone.

So, now that she felt she could trust her memories, she was sure she had not gotten into a fight with Susanna. She still didn't know who killed Susanna—but it wasn't her!

The killer had set her up to doubt her memories by removing the transparency film while she was unconscious and then turning her over and pulling her away from where she would remember passing out, and by smearing Susanna's blood on her hands and pressing her hands around the handle of the shovel to leave her fingerprints.

It was a devious frame job.

Ginger walked over to the area where Boot had found Susanna's body. It was quite possible that Susanna was already dead before Ginger even came into the cemetery. They had both been set up.

She would go to the chief in the morning and explain it all. Bring him out to the crime scene and show him where the flashlight had been stuck in the ground in front of her gravestone. Let him feel the sticky spots where the date of death transparency film had been temporarily attached to the gravestone.

What would he say then? It's all circumstantial?

Unfortunately, he'd be right.

A flash of lightning startled her, followed by a clap of thunder.

Ginger hadn't discovered any evidence that would nail the killer, but at least she'd proven to herself that her memories were accurate and that she was not going crazy.

But there had to be something else. Some evidence that the chief and his men had missed.

Susanna was a tall, strong woman. Marilyn, Kate, and Caroline were average height. Could they have pulled it off? Maybe, with great difficulty. Al or Bobby definitely had the strength to do it. Fredrick? Physically, maybe. Emotionally, no. Maybelle? Probably not.

But what if Susanna had tripped on something and fallen down?

Ginger searched beyond the crime scene tape, several yards outside the perimeter.

Another flash of lightning, followed quickly by a clap of thunder.

Ginger needed to hurry. She was probably about to get drenched. She could smell the rain coming.

Wait!

She could smell the rain.

And it smelled right.

It smelled exactly like rain!

Her sense of smell was back!

It was so exciting, but she still needed to hurry. And rain wasn't really the issue. It was the lightning.

A flash in the sky startled her.

She hurriedly searched the brush, and her flashlight caught a reflection. There was something shiny just under the ground cover. She rushed to it, braced the end of the flashlight under her chin and parted the foliage with her hands. There was silver-colored, heavy wire wrapped around the trunk of the small tree, about a foot off the ground.

She got up and hurried to the opposite side of the crime scene tape. This time she knew exactly what to look for, so it didn't take long to find it. Another small tree trunk with the same type wire wrapped around it. Ginger looked across to where she'd located the first wire-wrapped tree trunk. Between the two trunks, within the crime scene tape, was about where Susanna's body had been found.

Lightning struck and the thunder boomed. It was close. Ginger needed to get to a safe place, but all she could think about was how the killer had done it. He or she set up a trip wire for Susanna, and once she was down, flat on her face, they battered her head with the shovel. So, even though Susanna was tall and strong, it wouldn't have taken a lot of strength to do the job. Any of her suspects could have done it.

She studied the wire on the tree trunk and wondered if she could track down where the killer bought it. It looked like aluminum.

Another flash of lightning and thunder clap. She looked up. A man was towering over her, and she flinched.

"Ginger, what are you doing out here?" It was Boot Hornamer.

"Boot, you scared me half to death. I thought you were the killer."

"Well, if I was, I guess you'd be dead right about now."

"Don't say that. It's been a rough couple of days."

"Yeah, but we need to take cover from that lightning before we get fried."

"I know, but look what I found. The police missed it." She pulled the brush back with one hand and shined her flashlight on the tree trunk with the wire wrapped around it.

"I don't suppose you found something similar over there, did you?"

"Yes, I did."

"A trip wire."

"Yeah," she said. "When you found Susanna's body, you told me that it looked like somebody pushed her down on the ground and then attacked her with the shovel. I guess the only question is, if she tripped on this wire, shouldn't she have had bruises on the front of her legs?"

"Not if she was wearing boots—which she was. You know, a pair of them dress boots."

"Well, there you go."

"I'll report this to the chief."

She directed her flashlight back to the wire-wrapped tree trunk. "I can't believe he missed—wait, I see something else." She dug her fingers into the grass and pulled out something shiny.

"What is it?"

"It's an earring."

"Must be the killer's. If that's a real diamond, maybe the police can track it to the owner. Good job, Ginger." Boot took a small Ziploc bag out of his pocket and opened it.

She studied it. "It is a real diamond. Definitely."

"How can you tell?" He held out the bag and Ginger dropped the earring into it.

"Because it's mine." She shook her head, thinking that she might as well go ahead and turn herself in.

"You sure about that?" He held up the bag and eyed the earring inside it.

"I lost it Wednesday night. But I'm not the one who set up this trip wire, Boot. You know good and well I wouldn't do something like this."

He zipped the bag and put it in his pocket. "I know you wouldn't, but it don't matter what I think. The chief's gonna be all over you. You know he is. And you really can't blame him. I mean, this looks bad. Real bad. And the fact that you can't remember exactly what happened out here—"

"No, I found out that I don't have any memory problems. The killer tricked me into thinking that. And besides, this trip wire had to have been set up before Susanna ever called me.

Before she came into the cemetery. This is premeditated murder. You know I didn't do this."

Lightning.

Thunder clap.

Pouring rain.

"Let's get out of here," Boot said. "I'll wait 'til morning to tell the chief."

CHAPTER THIRTY-SEVEN

Saturday, 6:51 a.m.

*G*inger's eyes popped open. She glanced at the clock on the nightstand. The alarm would go off in a few minutes at seven. She had not fallen asleep until nearly three. When she'd made it back to Ginger Bread House and gotten in bed with Jane, her sleeping partner had been out cold, and Barb and Ethel were in their bed snoring a duet.

Her nose was picking up the scent from the sheets. Detergent and fabric softener. She held her arm up to her nose and sniffed her skin. Then she tasted it. Yes, her senses were back at full strength!

There were always a few guests who liked to eat breakfast early, and Ginger could already smell them. Not the people. The coffee—the aroma coming from the kitchen, down two hallways, and under the bedroom door. Oh, the magnificent bouquet. And her coffee cakes. Lovely. She tried to pick out the scent of each particular variety that was being eaten.

Lemon Crunchies . . . Pineapple Doozies . . . oh—one of the guests had apparently warmed up a Sweet Ginger Cake in the microwave with butter on top.

Wonderful!

Her phone rang. She fumbled to pick it up from the nightstand and dropped it on the floor.

"Somebody please answer their phone," Barb said.

"What's going on?" Ethel asked.

"Sorry. It's my phone." Ginger picked it up from the floor. "I've got it."

"Good morning, Chief. . . . Right now? The carnival opens at eight and I need to. . . . No, I don't have a problem with that. I'll be there in a few minutes. . . . Okay, bye."

Jane rolled over to her. "What was that about?"

"The chief wants to search my house," Ginger said.

"What's he looking for?" Jane asked.

"He won't tell me," Ginger said.

"Call him back and tell him he needs a warrant," Barb said.

"Why? I've got nothing to hide." Ginger got out of bed.

"What brought this on?" Jane asked. "Did he say?"

"No," Ginger said, "but it probably has something to do with what I found in the cemetery last night."

"When did you go to the cemetery?" Barb asked.

"After y'all were asleep." Ginger gathered clothes from a dresser and the closet.

"Ginger!" Jane said. "You went out there by yourself in the middle of the night? Didn't you learn anything from the last time you did that?"

Ginger said, "Well, what was I supposed to do—wake you up and drag you out of bed?"

"You could have." Jane said. "I would have gone with you."

"Well, anyway, it was worth it because I made some big discoveries out there." Ginger walked toward the bathroom.

"Like what?" Barb asked.

Ginger turned around. "I'll tell y'all all about it later. I've got to go meet the chief."

"Aw, come on. You've gotta give us something," Ethel said.

"Just say it fast," Jane said.

"Fine." She rattled it off. "I never lost my memory after all. Well, I did, but only for a few minutes. Susanna's murder was premeditated, and I found my diamond earring, but it makes me look even more guilty."

Ginger ran into the bathroom to get dressed. She could hear them through the door begging for details, but she didn't have time for that. She'd told the chief she'd meet him in a few minutes, and she was in no position to be making him angry.

CHAPTER THIRTY-EIGHT

Saturday, 7:27 a.m.

When she got to her house, the chief and four male deputies wearing gloves were standing on her porch. A small army of intruders, ready to rifle through her dressers and closets and cabinets—each and every personal space.

"What took you so long?" the chief asked.

"I made it as fast as I could." She hurried up the stairs and unlocked the front door.

The men rushed in.

Ginger called out to them, "Please be careful. I've got a lot of delicate things, and they're all valuable to me."

Elijah drove up and got out of his car, and she walked out to meet him.

He held out his hands and took hers. "Sweetie, are you okay?"

"They're rummaging through all my things." She felt her

eyes begin to well up. "I knew I had to let them do it, but I just feel so . . . violated."

"I'm sorry." Elijah took her in his arms. "But, it's gonna be okay. You're gonna get through this."

"Who called you? Jane?"

"Yes, and she told me about you going to the cemetery last night. I can't believe you did that. The killer could have been out there."

"I know. It was stupid. And since I found the trip wire, the chief—"

"Trip wire?"

"Yeah. The killer set up a trip wire for Susanna, so she'd fall down—"

"And be in a vulnerable position on the ground."

"Right."

"Why hadn't the police already found it?" he asked. "You'd think they would have been tripping over it."

"Because the killer cut it off at each end where it was wrapped around a tree. But now the chief probably thinks I was the one who set it up and that I went out there to remove the wire from the two tree trunks."

"When did you tell him about finding the wire? This morning?"

"No. I didn't tell him. Boot Hornamer did. He caught me out there in the cemetery. You know how he is, driving around at all hours of the night. I guess he saw the light from my flashlight."

"Boot Hornamer keeps popping up at the most interesting times. Have you ever thought that it might be just a little too coincidental?"

"You're suggesting that Boot is the killer?" She laughed. "Well, thanks for that. I'd rather be laughing than crying."

"But, really—what's his alibi? Maybe he had a motive. Have you ever looked into it?"

"Okay, you're giving me a headache. I don't know if I can deal with having another suspect."

"Well . . ."

"I just keep thinking that if I hadn't gone into the cemetery Wednesday night, I wouldn't be in this mess."

"You went out there because you were worried about Susanna—that she might have tripped and hurt herself."

"Apparently, I was right about that."

"But you're not the one who tripped her. You were trying to help her. I mean, it's true that if you had stayed home and left Susanna out there to fend for herself, you wouldn't have been attacked, but—"

"Sometimes it just doesn't pay to be your brother's keeper."

"Well, it's not supposed to pay."

"I know."

"You always try to do the right thing. It's one of the things I love about you."

But if Elijah knew that Ginger had entered Marilyn's apartment illegally and searched through her things, and that she'd paid the building cleanup guy five hundred dollars for dirt about Chuck, then what would he think of her?

The chief walked out the front door with one of his deputies. "Ginger, do I have your permission to search your car and everything else on the property?"

"Sure, go ahead. I've got nothing to hide." Suddenly, she felt a wave of sarcasm rumbling up from her belly like vomit, and she just couldn't hold it in. She shouted, "Why don't you search my bakery too? And what about Ginger Bread House? I could be hiding something over there."

Elijah stepped in close and spoke softly. "Whoa, that's enough, sweetie."

But she had to finish it. She yelled, "Why don't you just rip apart the whole freaking town!"

The chief looked like he was about to lay into her, but then he turned around and went back into the house.

The deputy began searching her car.

Elijah said, "Are you okay?"

"Yeah. Sorry about that."

"It's okay. I know you're extremely frustrated with all this, and I don't blame you," he said. "Now, what do you suppose they're looking for?"

"I have no idea. If I was guilty, I guess I'd know, and I'd be worried that they'd find it."

"I've got it, Chief!" The voice seemed to be coming from the back yard.

Elijah and Ginger ran around to the back of the house. A deputy was standing in front of Ginger's tool shed. The doors were open, and he was holding up something silver. The chief ran out the back door to the deputy and took the item from his hand just before Ginger and Elijah got there.

The other three deputies joined them.

"What have you got to say about this, Ginger?" The chief held it up. "It appears to be your trip wire."

"That's not mine, and you wouldn't even know about the trip wire if I hadn't discovered it. You and your deputies missed it."

"So, you were just helping us out when you snuck into the

cemetery in the dead of the night looking for clues that we missed?"

"No, I was trying to help myself—to prove that somebody else killed Susanna so you'd give up this crazy theory that I did it."

"Crazy theory, huh? And what if Boot hadn't come along last night when he did? Would you have even told me about this new evidence, or would you have removed the wire from the tree trunks, put your earring back in your jewelry box, and never told anyone?"

"Earring?" Elijah asked. "What earring?"

Ginger said, "You are determined to make me into a killer."

The chief smirked. "Well, if the earring fits . . ."

"Let me see that." She reached for the roll of wire.

The chief pulled it back. "Don't touch."

Ginger put her hands at her sides. "Okay, I won't. I just want to take a closer look."

The chief hesitated. "All right." He held it out for her.

She leaned in close, thinking that if this was the wire that had been used to trip Susanna, then it should look like it was unrolled and then re-rolled, and each end should look like it had been snipped off with wire cutters, and it should be scuffed.

Unfortunately, the wire passed all of her tests.

She smelled something—other than the aluminum—and moved in very close and took a quick sniff of the wire.

The chief yanked it away. "I told you not to touch it."

"I didn't," she said. "I just smelled it."

"And what did you smell?" he asked.

"I'd rather not say."

"Cuff her," the chief said to one of the deputies.

"Chief, is that really necessary?" Elijah asked.

The chief said, "Okay, forget the cuffs. Just take her to the station."

"I know who the killer is now," she said.

"There you go, Chief," Elijah said. "Ginger's figured it out."

"Okay, Ginger, who's the killer?" the chief asked.

"I'm pretty sure about it," she said. "I just need to do a little more investigating."

"You're stalling," the chief said. "Take her in."

The deputies walked away with Ginger. She heard Elijah begging the chief to give her more time.

One of the deputies put Ginger in the back seat of his patrol car, and he and the other deputies got into their cars and pulled away from her house. Ginger had never ridden in the back of a cop car. She wondered how many criminals had sat in the very spot where she was sitting and whether the seat had ever been disinfected.

She had leverage now, and she planned to use it. The chief knew that she smelled something on the trip wire, and that it was a clue, but she was not about to tell him what it was. He would have to release her if he wanted the murder solved.

CHAPTER THIRTY-NINE

Saturday, 8:03 a.m.

The chief drove to the courthouse, knowing he had Ginger right where he wanted her. He would extract a confession, close the case, and get all of the credit.

He smiled. He was in control, and it was gonna be a good day.

He parked and got out of his car.

Elijah came out of nowhere. "This is not right, Chief. You can't do this to her!"

Several people on the sidewalk heard him yelling at the chief and stopped to watch.

The chief saw the people staring and was embarrassed. "Would you like to go to jail too?"

Elijah lowered his voice. "She's so close to figuring it out. Can't you give her a little more time?"

"Look, Pastor, I know you two are in love, and that you're just trying to look out for her, but that's why you're not seeing things the way they really are. You know what they say: love is blind." He closed his car door and began walking away.

"Why can't you wait until the end of the carnival—or at least until after the cake judging this afternoon? Wait until after the prizes have been awarded—like you said you would."

The chief stopped and turned around. "That was before I had this new evidence. And, besides, a few more hours are not gonna make any difference."

"Not to you, maybe, but Ginger could solve the case. If you lock her up now, right when she was about to—"

"Ginger's bluffing. She just wants more time to try to weasel out of what she's done. But when you do the crime, you've gotta do the time."

"But what if you're wrong, Chief? It's gonna be awfully embarrassing for you. Humiliating."

"I'm not worried about—"

Elijah walked up close. "You know how popular Ginger is. You know how much people love her. If you throw her in jail, and then it turns out that she did nothing wrong, and in fact was only a victim, the people of this town are gonna hate you. And then, how long do you think you'll be keeping your job?"

"Are you threatening me, Pastor?"

"Not at all. I'm just trying to keep you from making a terrible mistake."

"Oh, you're just looking out for me, huh? Well, thanks, but I don't need your help." He turned and walked into the courthouse.

CHAPTER FORTY

Saturday, 1:20 p.m.

Ginger appreciated the fact that she had not been arrested, but the chief wouldn't let her go. He'd been grilling her in his office for four hours. She'd answered the same questions a dozen times. Elijah had been waiting in the receptionist's office, and around noon, he'd gone to Subway and brought back a sandwich for her. The receptionist brought it in, but the chief wouldn't let Ginger have it. Maybe he thought he could starve a confession out of her.

She'd given the chief a lot of information, but not the most important stuff, and she never revealed who she thought the killer was. She kept telling him that she needed to do a little more investigating. She didn't dare admit that she had no solid evidence. Her plan was to manipulate the killer and draw out a confession. But it would be tricky, and she knew that the chief couldn't pull it off. He was not capable of finesse. He would botch it, and the killer would walk.

He finally released Ginger and told her that he and his deputies would be there at the carnival, ready to arrest her the moment the baking contest was over. She'd be cuffed right in front of everyone and hauled off to jail—unless she delivered the killer before then.

She walked out of the chief's office, and Elijah said, "To the carnival?"

"Yes. It's nearly one-thirty."

As they left the receptionist's office, they heard the chief say, "I meant what I said, Ginger. Put up or shut up."

They took the stairs.

"I've got until the end of the contest," she said.

"He sure didn't leave you much time."

"That's okay. I can do it."

They ran out to Elijah's car and got in.

Ginger said, "Thank you for the sandwich."

"You're welcome." He started the engine.

"He wouldn't let me eat it."

"What?!" Elijah opened his door. "I'm gonna—"

She grabbed his arm. "We don't have time for that. We've gotta go."

He drove her to the carnival gate and she got out.

"It may take me a few minutes to find a parking spot, but I'll be in as quick as I can."

"I love you."

"I love you too, baby."

She closed the door and he drove away.

Ginger had easily recognized the scent on the wire that the deputy found in her tool shed: Chanel No. 5. And she remembered who she'd smelled it on in the past. The only question was whether she'd be wearing it today.

Ginger went to the Maybelle's Bakery tent. Maybelle was near the front, standing next to one of her employees.

"Beautiful day to win a baking contest," Ginger said.

Maybelle smiled. "We're gonna try."

She saw Caroline in the back of the tent and said, "Next year, you should enter your own cake, Caroline."

Caroline walked up to the front of the tent. "I'm not very creative when it comes to cake recipes."

Ginger smelled the Chanel No. 5 on her.

"Well, I'll see y'all at the contest," Ginger said. "Two o'clock."

"We'll be there," Maybelle said.

Ginger walked off. She was satisfied, thrilled to have solved the case.

She was headed toward the Coreyville Coffee Cakes tent when she heard Barb's voice behind her. "Ginger! Ginger, you've got to see this!"

Barb rushed up to her with a folded newspaper in her hand. By the time she got to Ginger, she was panting heavily. "Look at this."

"Easy, Barb. Give yourself a chance to catch your breath."

"One of our guests gave me this paper. Susanna's obituary. Read it." She handed it to Ginger.

"Okay."

Barb said, "It's true—about Kate Lake. Her mother was Susanna's half-sister."

"So Kate lied to my face." Ginger began reading the obituary.

"She must be the killer."

"No, I don't think so," Ginger said. "I wonder where the paper got this information? Susanna didn't have any living relatives—except Kate, if this is true. But Kate doesn't seem to want anybody to know she's related, so she didn't write this. I wonder who did."

"You suppose it was that woman you talked to at Susanna's bakery—what was her name? Dot?"

"Dot Harbington. Yes, that would make sense." Ginger resumed reading the obituary. "Yadda, yadda, yadda . . . Susanna's husband died before her . . . wait!"

Ginger looked up from the paper and stared at Barb. "Did you see what his full name was?"

"Chuck's?"

"I never knew this. I never heard anyone call him anything but Chuck."

"Well, yeah, but Chuck's just a nickname for Charles," Barb said.

"Yeah, I know that, but it says here that his full name was Sharon Charles Clampford."

"Well, parents do that sometimes. Name a boy after some woman in the family. Of course, kids always make fun of a boy with a girl's name, but—"

Ginger checked her watch. "I've got to go. It's almost time for the Sniff-Out." She hurried off.

Barb tried to catch up with her. "Ginger, what are you thinking? Is that a clue? Ginger, wait."

CHAPTER FORTY-ONE

Saturday, 2:00 p.m.

The contestants were sitting in folding chairs atop a twelve-inch platform behind the cake table. The bakers were lined up in the same order as their cakes, as Ginger had arranged them, from left to right: Bull Crawley, Cash Crawley, Bobby Boudreaux, Maybelle Rogers, Fredrick Marcello, Al Fenster, Kate Lake, and Marilyn Monastrovi. A picket fence had been installed ten feet in front of the cake table to keep the spectators at bay.

When Ginger walked out to the front of the cake table, everyone cheered. She smiled and waved to them. She spotted Caroline Rogers near the front of the crowd.

"Before I announce the three winners that our fine judges have selected for this year's bake-off, I will perform my annual ritual, called the Sniff-Out."

The crowd applauded.

"As you may have heard, my sense of smell had been on

the fritz for the past few days, which is one reason I am not participating in the contest this year."

A few in the crowd moaned.

"But fortunately, my sniffer is back in full swing as of this morning. Oh, and for those of you who are unfamiliar with the Sniff-Out, here are the rules: I am allowed to take as much time as I need to smell a cake, and then I must name at least two ingredients that are unusual or unexpected. You might ask, 'What if a cake doesn't have any unusual ingredients?' Well, then it's probably not going to win a prize."

Some people laughed.

"After I've called out two or three unique ingredients, the baker of that cake will give me a thumbs up or a thumbs down." She looked at the contestants. "And please be honest, people."

Most of the contestants laughed. Bull Crawley stuck out his tongue. Bobby Boudreaux shrugged.

Ginger went on. "I get one point for each cake that I sniff out correctly, and this year we have eight entries, so if I earn all eight points, then I will automatically win the first-prize trophy even though I didn't enter a cake."

People laughed and snickered.

"Just kidding," she said. "Y'all, the Sniff-Out is just for fun—and to make these talented bakers sweat a little, waiting to hear who won the trophies. So, here we go."

She picked up the plate with Bull's cake on it and sniffed it a couple of times. Other than the expected flour, sugar, vegetable oil, vanilla, etc., she detected a hint of some other interesting ingredients. "Bull, I'm picking up mustard powder . . . cayenne . . . and garlic."

Bull shook his head. He looked disgusted.

Ginger looked out at the crowd. "Is that correct, Bull? I need a verbal response." She looked back at him. "And remember, we're on the honor system here."

He smirked at her. "Yes, Ginger, you're right. I don't know how you do that."

The spectators applauded.

Next in line was Bull's brother, Cash Crawley. Ginger easily smelled the pickle juice and pepperoni bits and called them out.

Bobby Boudreaux's cake contained four types of sugar: granulated, powdered, brown, and coconut sugar. Also, a few drops of tequila and pear vodka.

Ginger sniffed out the remaining cakes and nailed every one of them, to the crowd's delight. But one of the cakes had an interesting smell that Ginger did not divulge to the audience—because it was a clue. The scent wasn't actually in the cake—it was on the cake plate: olive oil, with a touch of mint.

"Now comes the moment you've all been waiting for: the announcement of the winners. And I have the envelopes right here." She took them out of her pocket and held them up. "But I'm going to give you just a minute to talk among yourselves and tell your friends and family who you think the three winners are."

She walked to the side where the chief was standing and whispered in his ear, "I know who the killer is."

"For sure?"

"Yes."

"Great. Who is it?"

"I need you to set up a meeting in your office at three o'clock with everyone who was there Thursday night when you played the recording, plus Caroline Rogers."

"No, Ginger."

"Your deputies can inform them right after the contest winners are announced. Okay?"

"No. Just give me the name of the killer."

"Please, Chief. This is the only way I can get the killer to confess. Trust me."

He scowled at her. "So, everybody from the other night, plus Caroline Rogers. Got it. What about Bull and Cash Crawley?"

"No, I don't need them."

"Okay, Ginger, but this is your last chance."

"I understand. Thanks, Chief."

She walked back in front of the cake table. "Okay, folks."

The crowd settled down.

"Before I announce our winners, I'd like for you to give our judges a big hand." She pointed to them. They were standing together at the far left side of the crowd. "Those judges are extremely picky. It's very hard to impress them. They make their decisions based on many factors, such as aroma, flavor, after-taste, freshness, color, density, moistness, and much more. As they say, it's complicated."

Some people laughed.

Ginger went on. "So, it's a tough job, y'all—whether you're a baker or a judge. Okay, so the winner of the third-place trophy is," she opened the envelope and took out the card, "Bobby Boudreaux! Way to go, Bobby!"

The crowd cheered.

Bobby looked surprised, then overjoyed. "I can't believe it! I finally won a trophy!" He started fist pumping.

A young woman who worked at Ginger's bakery walked up to Bobby and handed him the trophy. He held it high above his head. You would have thought he'd won an Olympic medal.

Ginger said, "The winner of the second-place trophy is," she read from the card, "Kate Lake! Congratulations, Kate!"

Kate wasn't nearly as enthusiastic as Bobby. She probably had thought she'd walk away with the first-place trophy.

Once the cheers began to wane, Ginger said, "And now . . . the biggie . . . the best cake in East Texas in 2016, according to our expert panel of judges." She opened the envelope and took out the card. "Well, I'm looking at a name here, but I happen to know that, technically, this is not the correct name."

People murmured, on the stage as well as in the audience.

"So I'm going to announce the name of the person who actually created the recipe and baked the first prize cake: Marilyn Monastrovi!"

The crowd cheered.

Marilyn looked stunned. When the young woman handed her the trophy, she just smiled and stared at it as though she were hypnotized.

Fredrick jumped off the stage and ran up to Ginger. "Let me see that." He snatched the card from her hand. "Susanna Clampford? Oh." He handed it back to Ginger. "Sorry."

"Maybe next year, Fredrick," Ginger said.

His shoulders slumped. "Yeah. Maybe next year."

Some people from the audience were making their way up to congratulate the winners, but most were quickly dispersing, and Ginger knew where they were headed: to the tents of the winning bakers to buy the prized cakes. All of the bakeries had prepared dozens of their contest cakes, knowing there would be a run on them if they won a trophy.

Deputies were making the rounds, talking to each of the

contestants that Ginger had requested attend the meeting in the chief's office.

Elijah walked up to her. "What's going on?"

"I asked the chief to call a meeting in his office."

"You know who the killer is?"

"Yes."

He leaned in. "Who is it?"

She shook her head. "I'm sorry, sweetie. I don't want to jinx it."

"Can I be there?"

"I'll say yes because I'm running the show."

He smiled. "I can't wait to see it."

CHAPTER FORTY-TWO

Saturday, 2:56 p.m.

Ginger was standing at the side of the chief's desk, watching her suspects file into his office and take a seat in the row of chairs facing her and the chief. By three o'clock, all of the chairs were occupied. From left to right, there was Marilyn Monastrovi, Fredrick Marcello, Al Fenster, Maybelle Rogers, Caroline Rogers, Bobby Boudreaux, and Kate Lake.

Elijah was sitting in a chair in the back corner. Two deputies were stationed in the other back corner, near the door.

Ginger said, "I asked the chief to call this meeting so that I could identify Susanna Clampford's killer."

Al said, "Well, if you know who it is, just tell us."

"I had nothing to do with it," Kate said.

"Me either," Bobby said.

"Actually," Ginger said, "you all had something to do with it."

"What? This is stupid," Caroline said.

"Stop!" The chief stood up. "I want everyone to shut up and listen to what Ginger has to say, and if you don't behave, then I just might have to charge you with obstruction of justice."

"You can't do that," Al said.

"Try me," the chief said.

"Fine," Caroline said. "Let's just get it over with."

Ginger said, "Thank you, Chief. I'll start with Bobby Boudreaux. Bobby, you've got a terrible temper and sometimes you turn into a madman when you get drunk. You're liable to start throwing things or bite somebody's ear off."

"It was just the lobe." Bobby pointed to his. "And that was a long time ago."

Ginger said, "Yes, one night in Shreveport, right after you found out that Susanna had stolen your cake recipe and was selling it as her own."

"She even used the name I gave it," Bobby said.

"The Big Boy Chocko Cake," Ginger said.

"That's the best chocolate cake I've ever tasted," Maybelle said. "That's your recipe, Bobby? No, it couldn't be. That was Susanna's signature cake."

"Yeah, but it should have been my signature cake!" he said.

Kate said, "You expect us to believe that?"

"Bobby's telling the truth," Marilyn said. "It happened before I went to work for Susanna, but she told me about it a couple of years ago. I'm sorry, Bobby."

Ginger went on. "So, Bobby, Al told me that you got drunk in the hotel bar Wednesday night and started ranting and raving about how Susanna had ruined your life. Then you left the bar and nobody knows where you went—not even you—and the next morning you were wearing the same clothes as the night before. So, I thought, Bobby's probably the killer."

"I am not the killer," Bobby said.

"I know that now," Ginger said. "Al, years ago, you had a thriving restaurant in Marshall. But after you added a bakery to your restaurant, it began to pull customers away from Susanna, and she didn't like that one bit."

"She couldn't take it," Al said.

"I've heard the rumors about Susanna hiring a man to go to work for you, and how he put horse meat in your fridge and cockroaches in your flour."

"Yuck," Kate said.

Ginger continued. "Then she made an anonymous call to the health department. It ruined your business, and you had to start all over in a different town. Of course, these days, you've got a nice deli and bakery in Longview, but from what I understand, you're struggling financially."

Al said, "I'm gonna be fine, but it's been tough to recover from what she did to me. I hated that woman. But I didn't kill her."

"How do you know for sure that Susanna was the one who set you up? Did the guy ever admit that she'd hired him to plant the horse meat and the roaches?"

"I never got a chance to ask him. He disappeared. But I know it was her. No doubt about it."

"Well, maybe we can verify that right now," Ginger said. "Marilyn, I know this would have happened well before you went to work for Susanna, but did she ever say anything about it?"

Marilyn sighed. "Could we please put an end to this Susanna hate-fest? The woman's dead. I know that a lot of you people didn't like her, but—"

Bobby's face turned red as he shouted, "Didn't like her? Are you kidding me?"

"Okay, okay, we get it, Bobby," Ginger said. "But, Marilyn, if you know, you've got to tell us. Did Susanna really do that to Al?"

"Yes."

"I told you!" Al said.

Ginger said, "Marilyn, you and Susanna were very close."

"She was like a mom to me," Marilyn said.

"Yes," Ginger said, "she obviously loved you. I mean, she must have—she put you in her will."

Marilyn said, "How did you know about . . ."

Everyone in the room stared at Marilyn.

Ginger went on. "And when I found out about the will, I thought, gee, that might be a motive for murder if the two of you didn't love each other so much. Then I heard that Susanna's husband, Chuck, had been having an affair, and that she'd found out about it and murdered him."

Marilyn jumped up. "Susanna didn't murder Chuck. He died of an accidental overdose. Ask the police."

The chief said, "Please sit down, Marilyn."

She sat down.

"Sometimes the police get it wrong." Ginger glanced back at the chief. "No offense, Chief." She studied Marilyn's face. "And if the police are wrong and Susanna did murder Chuck, that would give you two motives to kill Susanna."

"What are you suggesting—that I had an affair with Chuck?" Marilyn asked. "That's the wildest thing I've ever heard. I don't know who's spreading these rumors, but they don't know what they're talking about."

Ginger looked at Al. "Al, why did you keep lying to me? First, you told me you were in the hotel bar during the time of the murder. Then you told me you'd gone to the gym. But that turned out to be a lie too—which really made you look suspicious."

"Yeah, but I explained where I was and why I'd lied about it."

"Yes," Ginger said, "you said that you were actually in the hotel parking lot, smoking a cigar."

"Al!" Maybelle punched him in the arm. "You told me you quit."

"I'm trying," he said.

"So how can I believe anything you told me?" Ginger asked. "And I wondered about you, Fredrick, because of the fact that you showed up at my house at ten o'clock on Wednesday night to expound on the joys of creating the perfect cake frosting. It's common knowledge that I spend a couple of nights per week at Ginger Bread House. So in hindsight, I wondered if you had come to my house to keep me there and make sure I stayed awake for when Susanna, or some partner of yours pretending to be Susanna, called me on the phone to lure me into the cemetery."

"Now, Miss Ginger, you know I wouldn't do that to you," Fredrick said.

She went on. "And I figured if you had a partner, it had to be Kate."

"No way," Kate said. "I had nothing to do with it."

"It wasn't much of a leap to think that Fredrick would

team up with his former girlfriend, who he's trying to win back."

"He's never getting me back," Kate said. "I'll tell you that right now."

"And Kate, you jumped to the top of my list when I learned that your mother was Susanna's half-sister—"

"I wish you'd quit saying that," Kate said. "It's a lie."

"Your mother was working in Susanna's bakery when she was pregnant with you—"

Kate crossed her arms "False."

"And Susanna was forcing her to work long hours until the day she had the baby—even though her doctor had ordered bed rest. Sadly, she died when she was delivering you."

Kate's voice sounded shaky. "None of that is true."

"Then I wonder why your mother is listed as Susanna's half-sister in this obituary?" Ginger grabbed the newspaper from the chief's desk and held it up.

Tears ran down Kate's face.

"I'm sorry, Kate," Ginger said. "I'm not trying to be mean, but I happen to know that you're in Chuck and Susanna Clampford's will. I suppose it was the least they could do for you. But after Chuck died, Susanna was preparing to change the will and take your name out of it. So, it's no wonder that you would want to kill her before she could do that."

"I don't know anything about their will," Kate said through her tears. "But it doesn't matter anyway because I don't want anything from that woman."

"So, you hated her," Ginger said.

"Yes!"

"It's understandable, considering how she treated you and your mother. She could have taken you in as a baby. She should have. But instead, she let them send you off to an orphanage."

"Stop," Kate said. Her face was red and her eyes were swollen.

"And Caroline," Ginger said, "your mother worries about you. She says you're a workaholic. So she's always pushing you to take some time off, maybe get out there and find a nice man. And you finally relented and told her you were going to start taking piano lessons."

"I did take piano lessons."

"Yes, you did. Two nights a week. You discovered that your old piano teacher was still around—the one who taught you when you were a kid—and you started taking lessons from her."

"Are you gonna tell my whole life's story?" Caroline asked.

"Your teacher had moved to Marshall, but that didn't stop you, even though it was an hour drive each way. And everything was just fine until she had to retire because of Alzheimer's. That was last August. But you just kept making those trips to Marshall twice a week."

Maybelle looked at Caroline. "What were you doing over there?"

Caroline glared at her. "Mother."

"That's what I wanted to know too—what you were really doing and why you were lying to your mom about it. I thought that maybe your old teacher had recommended a new one by the name of Chuck Clampford."

"I've never taken lessons from him," Caroline said. "I've never even met him."

"I figured you'd say that. But I talked to the man who

cleans the office building where Chuck's music studio was located, and he identified you, Caroline."

"He's lying," Caroline said. "I've never been there. I don't even know where it is."

"There's a lingering scent of Chanel No. 5 in Chuck's music studio on his sofa, and that same scent—although faint—is on the trip wire," Ginger said.

"What trip wire?" Maybelle asked.

"The killer set up a wire along the cemetery shortcut path so Susanna would trip and fall down, making it easy to attack her with the shovel. Once Susanna was dead, the killer cut it at both ends, rolled it up, and put it in my tool shed—to frame me. But it backfired because of my sensitive nose. There was a hint of perfume on the wire: Chanel No. 5."

"A lot of women wear Chanel No. 5," Caroline said. "That doesn't prove anything."

Ginger said, "So, I figured you were having an affair with Chuck, Susanna murdered him because of it, and then you murdered Susanna in the cemetery and framed me."

"I did not!" Caroline said.

Ginger said, "Yes, I had planned to declare you the killer at the end of the contest."

"I didn't do it," Caroline said. "You've got it all wrong. This is nuts."

Ginger continued. "But then, during my Sniff-Out, something jogged my memory, and my mind transported me back to the cemetery on Wednesday night. I saw the flashlight that someone had positioned on the ground, pointing it up at the date of death on my gravestone, which obviously should not have been there. And I remembered something I'd read in

Susanna's obituary, and then suddenly all of the puzzle pieces fit together perfectly . . . and I knew who the killer was."

Ginger looked at one face, then another, until Bobby yelled. "Who is it?"

Ginger stared intensely at Marilyn. "All of your workers at the bakery love you, Marilyn, and for your birthday, they wrote sweet little things on Post-it notes, like . . . " Ginger took out her phone and read from it: "'Happy Birthday, Sweets! You're the icing on everybody's day.' Isn't that nice?"

"Where did you get that?" Marilyn asked.

Ginger went on. "Here's another one: 'Happy Birthday! Your cupcakes taste like a symphony.'"

Marilyn said, "You broke into my apartment!"

Ginger continued. "I didn't notice anything out of the ordinary about those notes at the time. But then today, I was reading Susanna's obituary, which of course mentions her deceased husband, Chuck, and I was surprised to see that his full name was Sharon Charles Clampford."

"Ginger, please," Marilyn said.

"Sharon's an unusual name for a man, of course, and when I read that, I remembered that one of your sweet little birthday notes was signed by a woman named Sharon, and I realized that Sharon was not a woman after all. The Sharon who wrote that note was actually Chuck Clampford. Now, I don't know whether he was trying to conceal his identity or whether he was just being cute, but one thing's for sure: when he told you that your cupcakes taste like a symphony, he wasn't talking about bakery goods."

"Oh, my," Maybelle said.

"I mean, it made a lot of sense that he would use the term

symphony," Ginger said. "He was a classically trained musician, after all."

Marilyn looked distressed.

Ginger said, "Now, if Marilyn was having an affair with Chuck Clampford and she believed that Susanna murdered him, she just might have wanted to take revenge. So I wondered how Marilyn might go about it. Suppose that when Susanna held that meeting in Marshall a couple of weeks ago, she asked Marilyn to record what the other bakers were saying?"

Maybelle said, "No, I'm the one who recorded the conversation, Ginger, remember?"

"Yes, but Marilyn could have recorded it too," Ginger said.

"But I didn't," Marilyn said.

"So, Susanna hears the recording and gets upset that y'all weren't interested in selling your bakeries to her. But she likes the sound of your plot—not the part about killing her, of course—but the idea of luring me into the cemetery to kill me. She figures that after the murder, she can use the recording to throw suspicion on all of you. She needs help to pull it off, so naturally, she recruits Marilyn. But Marilyn decides to use Susanna's own plan against her. They attach a transparency film to my gravestone to make it look like a date of death has been carved into it. Then they lure me into the cemetery and draw me to a flashlight that is stuck in the ground pointing up at my gravestone."

"This is pure speculation, Chief," Marilyn said. "And none of it's true."

Ginger went on. "Then Susanna calls me on the phone to tell me she's walking through the cemetery to get to my house, drops her phone on purpose and then hangs up to make me think she's fallen and possibly hurt herself. So I rush into the cemetery to find her, and I see the flashlight and go to it. I think Susanna will be there, lying on the ground. But all I find is the flashlight, pointed up at my gravestone. I lean down for a closer look because my gravestone has a date of death on it, and I'm shocked by the sight. That's when Susanna comes up behind me and hits me in the head with the shovel. She knocks me out, but can't bring herself to finish the job and kill me."

"She's just making this stuff up, Chief," Marilyn said.

Ginger continued. "So, Susanna just wants to get out of there. Marilyn has brought her to my gravestone by an alternate path so that when Susanna takes off down the regular trail, she runs right into the trip wire that Marilyn has set for her. Marilyn picks up the shovel and pummels Susanna's head. It takes a lot of rage for Marilyn to kill her that way, but Susanna had murdered Marilyn's lover, so . . ."

"Chief! Make her stop this!" Marilyn said.

Ginger said, "Then Marilyn rubs Susanna's blood on the shovel handle and on my hands. She even places my hands around the handle for a moment so that my fingerprints will be on top of Susanna's blood. Then she flips me over on my back, drags me away from my gravestone, and removes one of my diamond earrings. Then she cuts the trip wire at both ends and rolls it up, leaving my earring next to one of the tree trunks that the wire was tied to. Finally, she plants the wire in my tool shed and puts just a drop of Chanel No. 5 on it."

Caroline jumped up and yelled at Marilyn, "You tried to send me to prison for murder."

"Sit down, Caroline," the Chief said.

Ginger said, "But then today, the entire scenario that I just laid out with Marilyn as the killer . . . well . . . it just fell apart."

"Ginger, what are you doing?" the chief asked.

"I'm getting there, Chief," she said. "Yes, Marilyn was having an affair with Chuck Clampford, but she didn't kill Susanna. And Susanna didn't kill Chuck, but he was murdered —by one of his lovers."

Marilyn blurted, "No! We were going to get married, okay? I was his only lover."

Ginger said, "Do you really still believe that after finding out about Chuck's music lesson appointment book? All of the students' names were written in code. Nobody, including the police, could decipher them. Why do you think he was hiding the names?"

Marilyn looked down.

Ginger said, "But I do know the identity of one of those students: Caroline Rogers."

Caroline shook her head. "Here she goes again."

Ginger said, "Here's what happened: you were taking lessons from Chuck on Tuesday and Thursday nights. Before long, you became romantically involved with him, and you wanted to see him more often, so one Friday night you drove to his studio, thinking you'd give him a nice surprise. But when you walked up to his door, you heard him inside with another woman, and they were making something other than music."

"That's just not true," Caroline said.

"The other woman might have been Marilyn. Anyway, you were furious, and on your way out of the building, you nearly ran over Jake, the guy who cleans the building every Friday night. He remembers you clearly. He said you looked extremely angry. Well, of course you were angry, because you trusted Chuck. You were in love with him, and you thought he was in love with you. But then you realized that Chuck was a dirty, lying cheater, just like your father—who nearly destroyed your mother. But you weren't gonna let Chuck destroy your life. No. You were going to destroy his."

Caroline stared at her mother and shook her head, probably wondering why Maybelle had told Ginger the awful truth about her father.

"So, during your next 'lesson,' the two of you had a few drinks together, as always, and at some point, he made a trip to the bathroom. Then you grabbed his bottle of pain pills—the ones he always took after sex for his back pain—and you crushed several of them and stirred them into his rum and Coke. When he came back out, the two of you finished your drinks and he slowly passed out. You knew that the combination of those pills and the alcohol would kill him. The stories about opioid overdoses have been all over the news."

Caroline said, "I didn't do that. It was probably her." She pointed at Marilyn.

"No, it wasn't Marilyn," Ginger said. "And you know how I know that? Because Chuck would never have been drinking with Marilyn because she doesn't drink, so she never would have had the opportunity to put drugs in his drink."

Marilyn was crying. "I can't believe you murdered him, Caroline. Why did you have to do that?"

"And then after Chuck was dead, Caroline, you prepared a fresh drink for him in a clean glass, poured most of it down the drain, and set the glass on his desk next to the Coke can and the open pill bottle. You wiped your fingerprints off everything you had touched, gathered your things along with the two used glasses, and left the building. It was late—maybe after midnight—and you knew that everyone else was gone, so you figured nobody would see you leaving. But once we tell the Marshall police to ask around about a red Prius with two bumper stickers—one for the Texas Tech Alumni Association and the other one for Maybelle's Bakery—I think they just might get a few hits."

Maybelle put her arms around Caroline.

Ginger went on. "And I was telling you a minute ago that during my Sniff-Out, something jogged my memory, but I haven't told you what that something was. As I was sniffing one of the cakes, I smelled a familiar scent—not in the cake—on the plate. A scent that had obviously transferred from the baker's hands. I was holding Marilyn's cake at the time, and it was no surprise that the plate had a slight hint of olive oil and mint because I remembered that the other day, Marilyn rubbed her special blend of olive oil and mint on my rough, cracked hands. She uses it as a skin moisturizer. Right, Marilyn?"

Marilyn stared at her blankly.

Ginger said, "However, at the time she rubbed the oil on my hands, my sense of smell was still not working. So, why was I remembering that scent? I hadn't smelled it at all when she'd rubbed it on my hands. I only knew what it smelled like because she told me."

Ginger glanced at Elijah in the back corner. He looked nervous, probably wondering if she was ever going to stop rambling.

She continued. "Then it hit me: the one time I'd smelled that exact scent before was in the cemetery on Wednesday night. When I leaned over to get a closer look at my gravestone, I smelled the plastic of the flashlight and something else . . . Marilyn's olive oil and mint hand lotion. It was on the flashlight. She surely would have worn gloves while handling the flashlight, the transparency film, and the shovel, but apparently, she'd handled the flashlight barehanded at some point earlier. And that was the clue that brought everything together for me and solved the murder—until . . . until I began to wonder why Marilyn would have been so careless about leaving evidence that would implicate her. She knew about my ultra-sensitive nose. So it didn't make sense for that smell to be on the flashlight—unless—"

"Somebody tried to frame me," Marilyn said. "A lot of people know about my homemade olive oil and mint hand lotion. I think I shared it with some of you at the bake-off last year."

"I thought they were trying to frame *you*, Ginger," Bobby said, "or Caroline."

"Marilyn and Caroline were the *backup* fall guys," Ginger said. "When I questioned some witnesses who had been at the back door of the hotel lobby smoking on Wednesday night, one of them said he saw Marilyn go into the hotel at eleven-fifteen, and then again at eleven-twenty-five. I thought at first that he was mistaken about one of those times—but then I realized what had happened. One of those was the real Marilyn and the other was an impostor. Some other woman was wearing a wig to make her look like Marilyn. Someone who was Marilyn's same height and size . . . like Kate."

"This is ridiculous," Kate said. "I need to get home to my bakery, Chief. I don't have time to be hanging around here all day long." She stood up.

"Sit down, Kate," the chief said.

She sat down.

Ginger said, "Kate, Fredrick told me that you tricked him into going to my house Wednesday night."

Kate glared at Fredrick, and he lowered his head and slid down in his seat.

Ginger continued. "You were using Fredrick to keep me occupied until you were ready for me. While I was in my kitchen talking to him, you slipped into my back yard, took the shovel out of my tool shed, and went into the cemetery and set up the trip wire. You positioned the flashlight on the ground and the attached the transparency film to my gravestone. Then you called Susanna, imitating my voice and spoofing my home phone caller ID, to ask her to walk to my house via the cemetery shortcut. You probably panicked when she didn't answer the call. You left her a voicemail, hoping she would just come, and not call back. It would have ruined your entire plot if she'd called me. But she didn't. And as she was walking along the trail, she tripped on the wire, and you jumped out with my shovel and beat her to death."

Kate said, "Chief, how many of her crazy theories do we have to listen to?"

Ginger went on. "Then, right after Fredrick left my house, you called me, pretending to be Susanna, and lured me into the cemetery. You put on a blond wig so that if I happened to see you before you hit me in the head with the shovel, I would think you were Susanna. And why wouldn't I? It was dark out there, and besides, I thought that she was the one who'd called me on the phone. Then you removed one of my earrings and placed it next to one end of the trip wire. You cut the trip wire at each end, rolled it up, put a drop of Chanel No. 5 on it, and placed it in my tool shed for the police to find."

Maybelle shouted, "Kate knows that Caroline always wears Chanel No. 5 because I mentioned it when we were talking at the meeting in Marshall."

"So what?" Kate asked. "I'm sure a lot of people knew."

Ginger said, "Your plan was to throw suspicion on Caroline, Marilyn, and me for Susanna's murder—which actually worked pretty well."

Kate applauded mockingly. "Well done. Now let's hear your scenarios for Maybelle and Al and Bobby."

Ginger said, "I suppose I should thank you for not killing me, Kate. I guess you didn't hate me as much as you hated Susanna. She had rejected you as a baby—her own blood—after working your mother to death. Then later, when Marilyn began working for her, Susanna practically adopted her. It was only at Chuck's insistence that you were added to their will, and after his death, Susanna was already talking about removing your name."

"Chuck was too good for her," Kate said.

"And you probably assumed that Susanna had murdered Chuck because of his infidelity—or to get her hands on his inheritance," Ginger said, "but you were wrong, of course."

Caroline began to weep loudly.

"But it wasn't about the will, was it?" Ginger asked. "It wasn't even really about Chuck's nine million dollar inheritance."

"Nine million dollars?" Bobby said. "Wow."

"The police investigators never could solve the mystery of the twenty thousand dollars in cash that Chuck had withdrawn from his bank account. Susanna never had access to the account until after he died, and she didn't know what he'd done with the cash. Her best guess was that he'd blown it on gambling. But that's not where the money went. Only you and I know, Kate."

"I don't know anything about it," Kate said.

"Chuck gave that cash to you so you could start up your bakery, didn't he? I know he wanted to help you because he forced Susanna to put your name in their will. But that wasn't going to do you any good for a long, long time—until after they both died."

Kate began to break down. "He was . . . the sweetest man. As soon as he found out he was gonna get the inheritance money, he called and asked if I would meet him. He didn't tell me about the money right away, though. He just wanted to hear all about what I was doing with my life. My plans and my dreams. I told him I wanted to open my own bakery someday. We started meeting for late dinners every week or two, and it was wonderful. He was so caring and funny. And then, after a couple of months, he told me he wanted to give me the money so I could open my bakery now. I was so excited, but I didn't really want to take the money. He insisted."

"So your relationship was strictly platonic?" Ginger said.

"Yes, of course. I'm twenty-two. He was in his fifties. He was a father figure. And when he died, I knew that Susanna had killed him. She killed my mother before I ever got a chance to see her. Now, she had murdered Chuck—the closest thing I'd ever had to a dad. So, she had to die!" She began weeping. "She had to die." Her voice lowered to a whisper. "She had to die."

Ginger turned to the chief.

He got up and signaled to his deputies, and they walked over to Caroline and Kate and escorted them out of the office. Maybelle followed them. Then the other suspects left. None of them said a word to Ginger. She had upset them all in one way or another. There might never be another bake-off.

Ginger said, "Thank you, Chief, for letting me do it this way."

The chief smiled and held out his hand. "We did it together."

She shook his hand. "I guess we make a pretty good team after all."

He released her hand and gave her a stern look. "But next time I've got a murder case, you'd better stay out of it."

"Yes, sir. I will." Maybe, she thought.

The chief walked out of his office.

Elijah walked up to her with a big grin on his face. "You did it!"

Ginger quickly put her hand over his mouth. "Shh! Don't let anybody hear you saying that. I need to make sure the chief gets most of the credit, or he might just decide to look into some of my . . . more questionable investigative techniques."

Elijah whispered, "Did you really break into Marilyn's apartment?"

"I have a one-word answer to that question: No."

He tilted his head. "And that's all I want to hear about it?"

"Correct."

"Well, it was amazing the way you nailed the two killers. Did you have it all planned out—the way you went after them, one by one?"

"Pretty much. Maybelle never had a major conflict with Susanna, so I didn't even bother with her. I wanted to eliminate Al and Bobby early on by showing that they had reasons to hate Susanna, but that they didn't have strong enough motives to kill her. Then I wanted to get Marilyn to admit that she was having an affair with Chuck by surprising her with that Post-it note. 'Your cupcakes taste like a symphony.'"

He chuckled. "She still didn't admit it, though, until you said that Chuck had been murdered by *one of his lovers*. That really got to her."

"Of course, the only reason I exposed Marilyn's affair was to get under Caroline's skin. The very thought of Chuck's *other* lover being in the same room with her made her start to crack. And after I insinuated that Chuck's music lesson appointment book was filled with the names of his many lovers, she probably realized that he'd never been in love with her, and that she'd thrown her life away for nothing."

"But how did you figure out that she'd gone to his studio on a Friday night and heard him inside with another woman?"

She grinned.

"You *guessed?*"

"I knew that the cleaning guy had seen her one night, and that she was angry, and that he only cleans the building on Friday nights. And Maybelle told me that Caroline was taking lessons on Tuesday and Thursday evenings, so—"

"You just filled in the blanks."

"Yep. And when Maybelle put her arms around her the way she did, I knew I'd convinced her own mother that Caroline had murdered Chuck."

"But what about Kate?" he asked. "Did you fake your way through that too?"

"No. Once I realized that the olive oil and mint solution had been rubbed on the flashlight to cast suspicion on Marilyn and that the Chanel No. 5 had been put on the trip wire to implicate Caroline, I turned my attention to Kate. I knew about her talent for imitating voices and about her being in

Chuck and Susanna's will. And Fredrick told me that on Wednesday night, Kate tricked him into going to my house. Then I remembered what that young man told me—the hotel employee who was smoking out back. He said he saw Marilyn go into the back entrance of the lobby twice—only ten minutes apart. So I thought, maybe one of those times it wasn't really Marilyn. Perhaps it was the killer, made up to look like her."

"But when you brought that up, it didn't seem to faze Kate at all," he said.

"No, but I had more. I knew she had recently opened her own bakery, and I wondered how she'd financed it. She's twenty-two, and her only living relative was Susanna. So when Fredrick told me that their breakup was a publicity stunt and that he was still in love with her, I figured he was loaning her money—until I overheard one of his employees in his tent telling him that the bank was about to repossess his fancy sports car. So I asked him point-blank if he'd given Kate financial help to open her bakery, and he said no. I believed him."

"So, the twenty thousand dollars that Chuck withdrew from his bank account—the mystery cash that nobody was able to trace—how did you know he gave that money to Kate to start up her bakery? Were you just guessing?"

"Yes. And I figured that Chuck quickly became the father she'd never had. But then Chuck died, and Kate thought he'd been murdered by Susanna—the woman who had literally worked her mother to death. It was just too much. Susanna had to die."

"Well, I'm just glad it's over."

"Me too."

"Yeah, it's been a long four days for you."

"Seemed like a month," she said. "But now that it's over, I've got something I need to tell you."

He looked worried. "What?"

"Yes."

Elijah hesitated. "Yes, what?"

"Yes, I will marry you, Elijah Bideman."

"Oh, sweetie." He reached out to hug her.

She held up her hand. "After you retire."

"Of course. That was the offer. We get married after I've built our house and retired. But what changed your mind? What happened to all that silly talk about how you're not good enough?"

"Yeah, I was worried about what the church people would say. But I've decided that I just don't care, because I nearly died in that cemetery the other night, and then I almost went to prison."

"I know."

"Life's too short to worry about what other people think."

"Amen."

"So, hurry up and build that house and retire, okay?"

"Yes, ma'am. I'm on it!" He saluted her.

"Good!" She saluted back.

He went in for a kiss.

The chief walked in and said, "Hey, this office is for official police business only."

Ginger and Elijah laughed.

Ginger said, "Okay, Chief."

She and Elijah walked out.

"I'm gonna give Addie a call and fill her in," Ginger said, "and then I need to go to Ginger Bread House and tell the girls what happened. They'll want to hear every detail."

"Absolutely. I'll drive you."

They walked up to the elevator, and Elijah pushed the button.

Ginger said, "And after that I'd like a nice dinner. Someplace where you can try to give me that ring again."

"Okay."

"Somewhere quiet, with a view," she said.

"Right."

"A picnic—where the two of us can gaze out the window at a beautiful landscape and talk about our future."

"And eat our favorite Subway sandwiches?" He grinned. "I know just the place."

THE END

Made in the USA
Coppell, TX
19 July 2025